Nestled within the hills of central Texas is a special ranch. A place that defies the laws of physics—that of time, space, and dimensions. It's a place where normal morphs with the paranormal and supernatural. A place that seems to know what a person's true desires and needs are, and then allows the right circumstances to occur to fulfill those wishes.

Welcome to the Gateway Ranch.

Your gateway to all things possible…

"Yes, I suppose so." Everything inside me hummed. His nearness was bewitching, and how could a man who worked around horses all day smell so good?

Hill country air. Leather.

Man.

Any anxiousness I'd felt about being trapped had washed away in the surge of longing for the cowboy. Primal, womanly instincts gripped me, urged me to kiss the pulsing spot in his neck, trail my tongue down to the dip where his shoulder and torso met, rest my hands on his chest and feel the beat of his heart and his strength.

God, I wanted to kiss him, and not that chaste kind we'd exchanged in the coffee shop. No, I wanted something like I'd seen in the movies, a soul searing lip lock that could only be experienced by two people destined for each other.

Gavin's heated gaze bore into mine. "Doesn't mean I can't do this, though."

As if he'd read my mind, he gave me exactly what I'd wanted.

This is a work of fiction. Names, characters, places, and incidents are either the product of the author's imagination or are used fictitiously, and any resemblance to actual persons living or dead, business establishments, events, or locales, is entirely coincidental.

To Be His
COPYRIGHT © 2020 by C.R. Moss

Cover Art by Casey M.
Three Flames Publishing
Publishing History
First Edition, 2020
Print ISBN 978-0-9854599-5-6
Digital ISBN 978-0-9854599-4-9

PUBLISHED IN THE UNITED STATES OF AMERICA

DEDICATION

To my writing cohorts ~ Thank you for your help on this story and for your friendships.

A big thank you to romance novelist, Terri Valentine, for mentoring me when I took my first steps in the world of publishing and showing me the way.

To CJM ~ Thank you for always being there for me. Your love and support of my goals keeps me going. Love you, Babe!

To Be His

a Gateway Ranch story

by

C.R. Moss

CHAPTER ONE

Of all days to run late.

Staring at the baristas behind the counter, I did my best to mind meld with the people in their navy-blue shirts, black pants, and orange aprons, mentally motivating them to hurry, knowing full well all the blame for my tardiness was on me. If I hadn't stopped at the campus's coffee shop near the art building for a double cafe latte with a dollop of whip, the rare, ten extra minutes I had wouldn't have been lost to standing in line.

I can't function, cannot live, without my morning fix though.

Especially today.

The first day of taking over a new-to-me class for a professor who'd gone absent without leave during the summer semester.

Rumors had swept through the art department that he'd gone on a bender down in the Keys. Others whispered he'd met a girl half his age and decided to find his groove again at a *playa* resort in Cancún. If pressed to hazard a guess and draw my own conclusions from the gossip bouncing around the halls of the university, I'd say inspiration struck the forty-something-year-old, and he'd gone off the grid to create his next masterpiece.

At least, I hoped it was only a matter of being a slave to his muse. It'd be horrible if something worse had befallen my co-worker, like getting drunk, lost, and arrested in some Mexican city. Or killed by a cartel.

Fleeting, precious seconds continued to tick by and disappear into the ether of the past. A song playing through hidden speakers that I'd been tapping my foot to ended, and another one began. The growing crowd of patrons waiting for their orders closed in, but I stood my ground, not budging from the prime spot near the pick-up counter where I'd be able to snatch my drink with ease and run out the side door. Every moment counted now.

"Professor Perez?"

Raising a hand and squeezing by some people, I said, "Here." Then as the employee, a young man I recognized from my fall semester's art history class the year before, stepped forward with my very large cup of caffeinated goodness, I reached out and took it from him. "Thank you, Jimmy." With my other hand, I pulled a dollar from an outside pocket of my canvas messenger bag and slipped it to him. I wasn't exactly a starving artist anymore, but I also hadn't forgotten what it was like to be one and trying to pay for an education on top of it.

"Thank you, Professor." He stowed the money in a pocket.

I opened my mouth to say welcome, but an all too familiar voice boomed in the noisy establishment, and I hesitated. Turning my head toward the loud patron, my stomach dropped, and cold dread trailed an icy fingernail down my spine.

Chadwick Hayes.

Asshole extraordinaire. Ex-boyfriend. The man I'd been all too happy to kick to the curb six months ago stood a few feet away, drawing attention to himself as usual.

Friends and family couldn't understand why I'd broken up with him. After all, I wasn't getting any younger, and he'd seemed like such a good catch—tall, built, handsome. He had a good job as a concierge at one of the high-end hotels in the city. He hailed from the northeast and had worked all over the country. His family was well off. Chad even received a modest trust fund check each month. We'd been together for seven years. Why throw it all away?

Because what looked good on paper didn't necessarily translate into a happy home life.

A shudder racked my body. My *abuela*, Lord love her, would have said someone was dancing on my grave.

Facing away from the group, I tried to shove all thoughts of the suave but arrogant asshole and what'd happened between us out of my mind. A name fell from his lips. My name.

Arianna.

Why was he talking about me? I didn't know, and definitely didn't like it. Despite my many clear and succinct statements to him that we were through, that our relationship was no more, the bastard kept resurfacing in my life like a bad rash.

Double checking that the cap on the drink was secure, I ducked my head, fed into the crowd, and slipped behind Chad to leave out the front door. It'd waste some valuable seconds having to sneak around the building to head in the correct direction, but if I could avoid Chad, then I'd sacrifice more of my prep time to do so.

Clear of the coffee house and the rest of the small, on-campus strip mall, I dashed across the lawn. With each slap of my sandaled feet on the ground, I imagined the images of Chad were being trounced out of my head. But it was harder to do than I'd hoped.

He'd looked even more put together than normal. The blond tips that had been part of his hairstyle were gone, allowing the richness of his light brown hair to be front and center. The locks had grown out, and now instead of a spiky haircut, he slicked it all back. He even sported some facial hair that made an anchor shape around his mouth and accentuated his dark brown eyes.

And that suit!

I wasn't into fashion, but the cut and fabric seemed expensive and fit his body quite well.

Why'd he have to look so damn sexy!?

After hurrying around the common area to the arts building and dodging some students lingering near the doorway, I swung open the door. A cool breeze from the air-conditioning, reminding me how hot and humid it really was outside, caused my long, flowing skirt to wrap around my legs. For a brief moment, I thought I'd trip and face plant onto the tile floor, but another door opened on the other side of the foyer and everything righted itself without further harm to my morning.

Breathing a sigh of relief, I adjusted the strap of the bag slung across my body, glanced at the coffee cup to check for spillage, and then ran to the stairs.

Up at my office, I found who I assumed to be the other professor's assistant waiting in the hall. "Tyler Chen?" I asked as I neared. "Hi. I'm

Professor Arianna Perez. Come on. We still have a couple of minutes before class starts. We can talk once we get into the room." Not bothering to duck into my office or wait for an acknowledgement from the young man clutching a clipboard loaded with papers, I continued heading toward the studio.

"Professor?"

Footfalls sounded behind me as he followed. "Sorry, Tyler. I know I'm running late. Let's get into class, make sure our model, Miss Kate, is ready to go, and then we can go over what we need to." I rounded a corner then opened the studio's door.

"But, Professor…"

Just as Tyler's words and his steps stopped, time seemed to slow, and the world before me drew a clear path to the model standing in the middle of the room.

The model wasn't Miss Kate.

Nor was the model a miss.

The almost naked man sported a white towel slung low around his hips. The material barely covered his butt. A fact that didn't seem to be lost on the students. Tittering females buzzed around and openly appraised him. The males perched on their stools and chairs behind their easels and canvases trying to look like they didn't care that they had tough competition in the room.

I, too, wanted to have a girly moment in which to sigh and fan myself as I appreciated the well-built man, but I had a job to do. First of all, I needed to make sure he fit the requirements to be the subject matter for the class. Though there wasn't a standard on how a person's body had to be to be a model, I still looked for certain aspects when it came to my sitters. Was he likable? From his easy-going manner and the way he seemed comfortable talking to the students, it appeared so. Did he look like he'd be able to handle being the center of attention and have the stamina for posing for almost two hours? Most definitely.

The model turned slightly, allowing a better view of his sculpted body. He looked as if Michelangelo had come back from the grave and chiseled him into a live version of the David statue, only better. This "David," whom I'd guess was six feet tall, had a nice, light golden-brown sheen to his body. Either he liked to be out in the sun or got spray tanned recently. His dark brown locks sat tall and thick and spiky on top of his head and morphed into a classic taper down the sides to his ears and nape. Perhaps he was ex-military? A close-cropped beard gave his chin line an angled, but strong and rugged look. The students were going to love sketching and painting someone with such anatomical definition. I know I would if I were in their position.

I wouldn't mind doing more with him than artwork. A little slap and tickle could do me some good. Get me back into the swing of dating finally.

"Professor Perez. I'm sorry, but I tried to tell you. We had a model change," Tyler said, breaking me from my thoughts and bringing the world back into real time.

Glancing over my shoulder at the assistant, I smiled. "It's all right, Tyler. I didn't give you much of a chance to." I looked back at the man, not having much luck dispelling the thoughts about the erotic things we could do together. "He looks like he'll do fine for what we need. Do we have a name for our subject matter?"

Tyler stepped up beside me and consulted his clipboard. "His name is Gavin—"

As the assistant spoke, the model turned our way. His mouth eased into a knowing, playful grin, and he winked. The eyes and the smile reminded me of someone I used to know.

"Bishop," I finished Tyler's sentence, then whispered, "Little G."

"Pardon? Do you know him?"

Feeling like a pervy old lady, heat blossomed in my cheeks. I spun to face the opposite direction to hide my reaction from the bulk of the students and

Gavin. "Used to. A long time ago. Let's go over to the instructor's table and get settled." I scurried along the perimeter of the studio over to a folding table. After removing the bag from around my body and placing it on the hard-plastic surface, I planted my hands on either side of it. Keeping my focus down, I took a few deep breaths.

Alarm didn't go off. Running late. Chadwick. Now a blast from the past.

A gorgeous blast from the past.

"Are you all right, Professor?"

"Yes. I'm fine. It's been quite a morning."

To say the least.

Closing my eyes, I took another deep breath.

Little G. Except he's not little anymore.

"Hello, Arianna."

Oh, Dios.

The sensual richness of his baritone voice sent my heart racing and made my knees tremble. Slowly, I opened my eyes and raised my head. Up and up I moved my gaze.

Yes. Six feet of pure male.

His nearness and overwhelming male energy and power kindled feelings in me I hadn't experienced in ages, years even. It'd been so long since I'd been magnetically attracted to someone, I'd thought I'd never enjoy such a reaction again. Clearing my throat, I pretended to be unaffected by his presence. "Gavin Bishop. It's been a while." I prayed he couldn't tell that I was completely captivated, that my heart fluttered like mad, and my knees wobbled.

"Twelve years and a few months." Another grin ruffled his mouth and faint lines crinkled around his deep blue eyes. He chuckled. His chest muscles rippled with his breaths and laughter.

I clutched the side of the table with one hand to keep my balance and not swoon, then looked at Tyler. "I used to babysit him and his younger sister, Cassady, until his family moved." I focused back on Gavin. "When you were what? Eleven?"

"Fourteen."

"Yes. Right." I'd worked for his parents for almost five years starting in my senior year of high school and up through my first four years of study at the university. Part of me hoped I'd correctly remembered a larger age gap between us so that my fired-up libido would be doused with cold reality. No luck there. He was still within my "ten years either way" age range preference for dating.

"Professor? We should get started." Tyler tapped his watch.

I nodded. "You filled in Mr. Bishop on how the process works?"

"Yes."

"Yeah," Gavin said as well. "He went over how many poses there'll be along with the timing of each."

"We'll need a combination of sitting and standing positions and make sure you rotate. You can't just face one section of the room the whole time." I opened my bag and pulled out a sketch pad followed by a box of graphite drawing pencils. If I had a chance, I planned to do a quick sketch of him.

"All right. Whatever you need." Gavin appeared surprised at the supplies.

"Everything okay? Any questions?" I opened the pencil container and then flipped the book open to a blank page.

"Sure. Everything's, um, great. Do have a question, though." He leaned toward me and Tyler. "Do I have to show, you know, my parts?"

Tyler coughed as if trying to cover up a laugh of his own.

I shook my head. "No. If you've brought a thong, you can wear that. Or if you've come up with some poses that strategically hide your genitals, that's fine, too."

"How 'bout props?"

"As long as they don't obscure main features and impede a student's ability to create, that's fine. I need you to be comfortable as well as provide a good anatomical learning experience for my class."

With a nod, Gavin went to the dressing screen set up in the corner of the room. He disappeared behind it.

Tyler brought the students to attention while I found a discreet spot to sit. "We'll open with three gestures at two minutes each," Tyler announced. "Then we'll break for five minutes. Three short poses will follow at ten to fifteen minutes in length for each. Before we head into the long poses, we'll break for fifteen minutes at which time if you want to switch mediums you may. All phones and recording devices are now to be switched off and put away." The assistant moved to the side of the room. "Mr. Bishop, when you're ready."

Gavin strolled out from behind the screen, the towel still wrapped around him, but this time a worn, black Stetson with a thin, braided leather hatband sat on his head. He took position in the center of the room, holding onto the towel on one hip and resting his other hand on the side of his waist.

Tyler called start, and the class went to work creating. For Gavin's next pose he moved his hand from his waist to the back of his head and bent his knee, and for his third gesture he placed his fingertips on the front brim of his hat and dipped his head.

With each of his changes, I switched to a different part of the room to observe my students. It wasn't lost on me that Gavin seemed to be following where I went, always keeping his gaze trained on where I was.

Even in his sitting poses or when I managed to move and have his back to me, he seemed able to turn his head and keep me in his sights. But it was his last pose that really had me wanting to run out of the room and lock myself in my office, away from his smoldering gaze and virile sex appeal.

He'd grabbed a chair with a solid back, spun it around and straddled it. As he sat, the towel fell open, but Gavin immediately, and to the dismay of the female students if their groans of disappointment were any indication, covered his crotch with his hat.

"Sorry, ladies," he said with a teasing lilt in his voice. "Only my special lady gets to see all of me." Once again, he winked.

At me.

As quiet commentary ensued, and several students glanced my way, I wished the floor would open and swallow me whole. *No*, I wanted to shout, *we're not an item!* I doubted they'd believe me, though.

Gavin settled into his last pose, one hand grasping the top of the chair as he leaned back. The stretch and elongation of his form became more pronounced when he swung his other arm up into the air, curving it so his hand and fingers extended over his head. Holding himself in place, he lowered his eyelids to half-mast and tilted up the corner of his mouth.

His placement reminded me of a bronco rider, but his expression, still trained on me, was all "come hither to the bedroom."

I did a quick sketch, replacing the chair with a horse and putting a lasso in the hand above his head. A part of me wished the long pose could go on for another twenty minutes so I could add in the fine details of his muscles and get all the shadows and nuances. But the other part of me was thankful when the class was finally over.

A glacial-like shower's definitely in order now.

After cleaning up, fielding questions about the other professor from the last few students who remained behind in the classroom, and saying good-bye to Tyler, I went over to the folding table, picked up my cup, and took a sip.

"Damn it. Cold."

"Let me take you out for coffee. My treat."

Startled, I almost dropped the cup. "Oh. Gavin. I'd thought you'd gone." I swept my gaze over him.

He was now dressed in a pair of black cowboy boots, blue jeans held up with a black belt and large silver buckle, and a blue-green short-sleeved plaid shirt. The top three buttons were left undone—a teasing reminder of the beautiful body that'd been on display, making the outfit almost seem out of place on him.

Glancing at my cup, I sighed. All that time and effort to get it, and I'd never drank it. Looking back up at Gavin, I wondered if it'd be a good idea to go somewhere with him. Students and faculty liked to gossip. Then again, the rumor mill was probably already in full effect as it was.

And I really wanted some coffee still.

"Sure. Let's go."

CHAPTER TWO

Less than twenty minutes later, we settled at a table in a quiet corner in the same café I'd been in earlier. He had his back to the wall and a view of the place, but I didn't mind. He'd said he enjoyed people watching. As for me, I liked facing away from the entrance. There'd be less chance of Chad noticing me right away should he return.

I placed my palms against the hot cup of coffee Gavin had bought me. Not because I was chilled but to help keep me grounded as I talked to the kid who'd grown into one fine looking man. "Little G. Of all the places to see you again after over a decade. The class I unexpectedly had to take over."

"Yeah, how 'bout that," Gavin said without any inflection of inquiry.

The statement had a tone of swagger, charm. Part of me wanted to leave. I'd had enough of that kind of cockiness to last me my whole life, but I also had to admit curiosity. Why after all this time had he come back? I stayed put hoping to find out.

"You're beautiful." The start of a charismatic grin tipped up the side of his mouth. "As gorgeous as I remember. Even better than Elena Montero de la Vega."

The name sounded familiar, but I couldn't place it. "Who?"

"Sorry. She's a character in the Zorro films. The actress. Something… Something Jones. Can't remember her full name at the moment. Anyway, Elena's always reminded me of you."

Once again, my cheeks grew hot. I wondered if I'd burn my fingers if I touched my skin. "Thank you. You've grown into one hell of a handsome man yourself." Realizing what I'd blurted out, a small gasp escaped me. "Sorry. That was a bit brazen to say."

Gavin chuckled, and his smile widened. "I don't mind."

I dropped my gaze and brought the cup to my lips.

"I've worked hard to be able to make a good impression," he added.

That's evident.

The switch to my arousal kicked on, flooding me with desire, to the point my hands started twitching a little. Carefully, I placed the cup back on the table. "I'm sure you're swimming in a sea of eligible, single women. Probably have some who aren't so single chasing after you, too."

"True." He gave a slight shrug of his shoulder. "I don't mean to sound cocky, but, yeah, I could have my pick. Thing is, there's only one woman I've ever really wanted." He reached out and touched my forearm.

A look of adoration and something else, lust maybe, settled in his gaze.

"Twelve years, huh?" I asked, hoping to change the highly charged atmosphere around us to something more comfortable. Sitting back in my chair, I drew the coffee cup toward me, thus pulling myself from his touch.

"Mmm-hmm," he replied.

The hum stretched across the small distance to my ears and burrowed into my core, touching me on an intimate level. I couldn't help but wonder if he made that kind of sexy sound when he made love.

Wouldn't mind finding that out.

Stifling a gasp, I drank some more of the brew to cover any expressions my face possibly portrayed.

What the hell has gotten into me? He was a kid. One I'd babysat. Wouldn't that be wrong? Incestuous-like? I peeked at him over the rim of my cup. Gavin smiled and scratched the stubble along his jawbone. No. He was an adult and *not* all that much younger than me. A non-relative. A *man* I had to get to know.

"Yeah, twelve years," Gavin continued. "I gather in that time you went through your graduate studies so you could teach. Bet you've settled down as well."

Nodding, I put down the drink. "After you and your family moved to California, I went into a Master's of Fine Arts program followed by PhD classes. Fortunately, I was able to start working at the university as an undergrad and then stay on as a professor. As for settling down, no. I just got out of a relationship a few months ago."

"Sorry to hear that."

I cocked an eyebrow. From the way his eyes lit up when I mentioned my relationship status, I doubted he was anything near sorry. "What about you? What brought you back to Texas?" A part of me wanted to ask why he hadn't tried to contact me before now. I mean, if he thought about me like it seemed he had, then why not track me down?

"A job. I'd started working on ranches in California as a teenager. My cousin's wife got a job offer on the east coast. She couldn't pass it up, and my cousin suggested I put in for the wrangler position he was vacating at Gateway Ranch about an hour west from here. I did and got the job. That was a while ago.

"Then a friend of mine was joking around with me about becoming a model and mentioned the need for them at the school. I figured, why not. I could use a change of pace now and then and the extra cash. So, I applied and was accepted. When I learned you were one of the professors, I was ecstatic. You know, I'd tried to find you before now, but the numbers my parents had for you weren't yours anymore, and they'd lost touch with your parents."

His statements sounded rushed, like he'd rehearsed what he'd say when he met me. That, or he happened to be anxious. And, if the man who oozed confidence was nervous, I wasn't going to point it out and make him feel even more awkward. "Well, it's been a long time. I obviously don't live where I used to when we all knew each other. I've changed emails since back then, too. My parents have moved a few times, as well. They're down in Galveston now as is my *abuela*."

"How is your grandmother?" he asked with a visible shudder. "You, um, haven't acquired any of her, um, skills, have you?"

I chuckled, remembering how skittish he'd seemed when she *read* him at a neighborhood block party. In fact, most people found sweet, unimposing *abuela* Chavela startling direct when she delivered messages from the other side. "Are you still freaked out about her psychic abilities?"

"Hey, I was a kid. It was weird to have a woman, who resembled an older version of you, tell me stuff about my granddad no one knew but me. But, no. Not exactly freaked out anymore. Let's say, cautious. And, get this. The ranch I work at? It's haunted. I think your granny would have a field day there."

"Yeah, she probably would, and to answer your question, my *skills*, as you call them, haven't developed as my *abuela* thought they would. Mostly I just feel stuff. Like a heightened sense of intuition. I never worked on honing those abilities to make them strong. Didn't want to scare people like *Abuela* could. But when it comes to my art, it can be helpful."

"Chavela ever meet your most recent ex?"

I shook my head.

Gavin hummed in acknowledgement as he appeared to scan the area behind me. He shifted in the chair. "I'm glad we've managed to reconnect."

"Yes." I said with a smile, feeling surprisingly good about the situation. An attractive man who'd had me in his thoughts and wanted to find me? The knowledge was intoxicating. "Between working the wrangler job and being my class's model, do you have time for anything fun?"

"I volunteer with the local search and rescue organization. When I started working on ranches, I became certified in First Aid and CPR. I found I enjoyed the courses and started working with rescue departments. When I came back to this area, I decided to continue doing the same. Being on the ranch and donating my time and effort to search and rescue is hard, demanding work. It's rigorous, but it's also rewarding. The modeling almost seems like a break from the craziness that is my usual workday."

Explains why he's so fit, I thought. "Ranch and rescue work. Doesn't sound like it leaves much time for anything else."

He shrugged, once more seeming to focus on a point somewhere behind me before focusing on me again. "It's all right. I enjoy helping others, keeping people safe. I feel I'm a good listener. People love to tell you their stories when they feel you're a captive audience. So, tell me, what's the deal with your ex? Was it tough calling it quits?"

Should I go down that rabbit hole with him? Especially considering we'd only become reacquainted a little while ago? But then, sometimes talking to a stranger, or a *long time no see* acquaintance, was easier than speaking to someone close and familiar. I weighed the pros and cons of discussing Chadwick with Gavin. The earnest expression on his face, as if he truly was sincere in wanting to know what I had to say, broke my wall of silence. Words tumbled from my mouth.

"Chad and I weren't serious when we first started dating. Not monogamous. He'd been seeing another woman. I'd been hanging out with another male friend. But then after a couple of months, our relationship developed into something more. We'd decided to become exclusive, and after about a year, we moved in together. Then as time went on, he began to change."

Gavin raised a brow and leaned toward the table. "How so?"

I drank the last of my coffee to give myself time to gather my thoughts. Thinking about that period in my life didn't make me all warm and fuzzy, which made me dislike remembering it, let alone talk about it. "I seemed to see less and less of him. He helped me get a part time job at a gallery. Both of us thought it'd give me a better chance of getting a show there. Then Chad started making more money. His personality seemed to change. I thought it was the stress of his concierge job or something until—" I took a deep, shaky breath and clutched the empty cup that'd I'd placed back on the table.

"Ari?" Gavin pried one of my hands from the container and squeezed my fingers. "We don't have to talk about it if you don't want to."

"I don't want to, but I think I need to." No one knew what had gone down between the two of us. Not my friends or family. I'd been embarrassed. Ashamed. Thought his abuse was all my fault until I convinced myself that wasn't true. Looking back, I realized I should have confided in someone. Maybe even seen a therapist. Learned to fight back.

"Chadwick had become verbally and emotionally abusive," I finally admitted. "I made excuses for his behavior. Then about a year ago, he hit me for the first time. Afterwards, he was real apologetic about it, did the whole *aren't I charming, I'll change* routine. He was good for about a month, yet his personality grew worse. He became more arrogant, narcissistic. Like he thought he was God's gift for everything under the sun, and that he owned me like a piece of property.

"Through various acquaintances, I'd learned he'd been cheating on me with multiple women. I went to one of the clubs he likes to frequent." An annoyed snicker escaped me. "According to him he *must* go clubbing because of his job. It helped to make and keep contacts." I shook my head and released a burst of air through my nose. "It was there that I saw him with one of the girls. I took pictures and left. When I finally gathered the nerve to confront him and show him the evidence, he hit me again. Hard backhand to the cheek. That's when I kicked him to the curb. Got him out of my life. Except he hasn't seemed to catch on that we're done."

Gavin sat back and rubbed his chin. "He's still bothering you?"

Nodding, I continued to breathe deep to allay my anxiety. "Yeah. Unfortunately."

"He sounds like a jerk. If you were mine, I'd treat you like a queen. I'd do anything I could to keep you safe and free from harm."

"If I were yours?" God, how I wanted to believe that a man would do that. Be a true gentleman, someone who would treat me right, someone I could trust not turn into a pig. Even if Gavin spoke the truth, there were other factors to consider. "You do remember there's an age gap between us, right? That I'm older than you?"

He lifted a shoulder again. "So? We're both adults. *Consenting* adults. I hated that my family moved, and I couldn't see you anymore. That I only had you in my fantasies."

"Wait. What?" This time I couldn't hide the surprise on my face. My hands jerked, almost causing me to upend the cup. "You... You fantasized about me?"

"All the time." He chuckled, and pink tinged his cheeks. "I thought you were the prettiest woman I'd ever seen, and I was a hormonal teen. I wasn't joking before when I said you're beautiful."

Compliments. Wants. Desires. The claims coming from him made my breath catch on such an intense wave of yearning it almost hurt.

Oh, Lord, what kind of spell is this man weaving over me?

"I appreciate the sentiment, but like I'd said, you could have your pick of women. Why would you want an older lady with a few extra pounds on her frame?" Under my breath, I couldn't stop myself from adding, "Chad used to say no man wanted a chubby-wubby."

Gavin pursed his lips then huffed. "We've already established that Chad's a tool. Me? I think you're perfect the way you are. You don't need to lose a pound." He smiled. His gaze softened. "God, I really want to kiss you."

Stunned by his admission, I was at a loss for words. Part of me wanted to ask him why? Why did he want to kiss someone like me? Another part of me didn't care and just wanted to make out with him. But instead of asking or making a move, all I could manage to say was, "Really?"

"Yeah."

Before I knew it, he leaned across the table, gently palmed my cheek and placed his lips on mine. Hungry desire flooded me. I couldn't deny my body's response or the fact that I was seriously attracted to Gavin. Despite my logic and attempts to protest, I wanted to be his. I wanted the kiss to deepen, but luckily, I had enough wits about me to not go crazy with the public display of affection.

Then, as quick as it started, it ended. He sat back, taking any decisions I might have had to make out of my hands.

"Thank you," he said. "I've wanted to do that for ages."

More heat blossomed in my face. I couldn't believe how much I'd been blushing. His attention and presence made me feel like a silly, teenager in the throes of my first crush.

"Do you ride? I'd love for you to come out to the Gateway Ranch and go riding with me."

"Yes. I mean, I've ridden in the past. I'm sure it'd come back to me once I was in the saddle again. Going out on the trails sounds like it'd be fun. I'd lo—" My ringing cell phone stopped my acceptance of his offer. Glancing down at the screen, I read: Chadwick.

The heat in my skin grew and not from a bashful or self-conscious reaction as had been happening. This time my physiological response came from anger. How did Chad always seem to know exactly when to bother me? His persistence in trying to get me back pissed me off. After all, I'd dumped him. He'd acted as if he'd wanted to be rid of me. Why was he still popping up in my life? Turning in the seat, I looked around the café. It was almost as if he'd been watching and knew exactly when to interrupt.

"Arianna? What is it? Your face is starting to look as red as Santa's suit."

I forced myself to take a deep breath and calm down. Righting myself in the chair, I gazed at Gavin. "As my *abuela* likes to say, 'speak of the devil and he appears.' It's my ex trying to call."

"You going to answer it?"

Shaking my head, I said, "No. He should know better. He shouldn't be calling me at all."

"What does he look like? This way I can help keep an eye out for you."

Remembering how I'd seen him before class started, I described him.

Gavin sat back then looked around the establishment, though it seemed as if he wasn't seeing what was in front of him. "Is Chad into something more? Something other than being a concierge?"

"What do you mean? Like having a hobby or activities outside of work?"

"More in the way of side-line business dealings that might not be on the up and up."

"Not sure." She gave a slight shrug. "Like I said, he wasn't around much, and when he was, he was bragging about himself, the clients, and the connections he happened to be making. The clubs and parties he'd been invited to. He'd gone on some quick trips to Vegas to visit a sister hotel there. I don't remember him talking about doing anything on the side. Why?"

"What you've been saying. It got me thinking. You've said he's changed. You seem skittish when it comes to him. I got the feeling there might be something more going on with Chad." He shook his head and waved a hand. "Aah, chalk it up to the shows about Las Vegas and the mob I've been watching. Maybe it's my imagination working overtime. Forget I've said anything."

"Done. I'm more than happy to forget about Chad." With a smile, I looked at my phone again. No voicemail. Good. Then the numbers on the home screen registered. "Geez, is that the time? I have another class in a half hour that I still have to prep for. I'm off tomorrow. I can meet you out at Gateway Ranch mid-morning, if that's all right. I'll find the information for the location online."

"That's perfect. I'll see you then."

I rose and hurried out of the café. On the way back to the building, I realized how nice it would be to escape the city for a few hours.

To go somewhere Chad wouldn't think to find me.

A girl could hope.

Right?

CHAPTER THREE

The morning turned out to be beautiful. One of those rare summer days with below normal temperatures that hinted at cooler times to come and made for wonderful riding weather. Once I was off the outer loop and on the state highway heading out to the ranch, I rolled down my car windows and breathed in the fresh country air. A bright blue sky studded with fluffy white clouds created a nice backdrop to the tree-lined, rolling hills. Living in the city and not venturing out enough due to work and other life responsibilities made me forget the magnificence of nature in my "backyard."

I needed the time away, even if only for a few hours, to relax and recharge my batteries. Having no disturbances out in the almost middle of nowhere would be wonderful, especially since Chad kept trying to reach me before I left. To ensure that my respite started as soon as possible and there were no more calls from him that I had to ignore, I pulled over to the side of the road, found my phone, and turned it off, then resumed my travel.

Just over an hour later, I navigated along the narrow-paved road with fields and bush and tree covered hills and mounds on either side, and having given up listening to the radio, heard some of the sandy dirt crunch beneath my tires. Soon, I banked into the entrance of the ranch, winding along the ecru-colored dirt lane up to the stone and wood buildings, and parked near a pool.

After exiting my vehicle, I admired the beauty of the ranch and realized the summer heat had decided to make a return. Fanning myself, I looked around. Some of the guest cabins were made of stone, some from wood, both styles which matched the house up the embankment and the tower behind it. Lush greenery surrounded everything beneath the beautiful sky.

Compared to the city, the area was super quiet. A peace filled my soul, as if the energy of the ranch wrapped me in its arms and said, "Everything will be all right." Sighing, I sent out a wave of gratitude for the serenity that'd descended upon me. I hadn't felt wholly all right, completely safe, since before I got messed up with Chad.

Gravel crunched nearby. I turned toward the sound and waited for a dark-haired, middle aged man with a cowboy hat in his hand to approach.

"Hello, miss. Welcome to Gateway. Name's Kent. Can I be of help?"

"I'm here for Gavin Bishop. We're going riding together today."

He cocked an eyebrow and plopped the hat on his head. "Sure thing. He's fillin' in some holes near the main lodge." Kent tipped his head in the direction of the large buildings. "Seems one of our resident ghosts likes to dig. Our ol' gardener, Harold. Died tragically. Poor fella. But don't try to tell Gavin who's diggin'."

"He doesn't think the holes are from the ghost? What about you?"

"Got me. Lots of strange happenin's on this ranch. Could be him. Could be any number of critters. Come on. Follow. I'll bring ya to Gavin."

We strolled up the hill along a path carved out under a tree and at the top, a shirtless Gavin pounded the ground. He glanced real quick our way. "Hey, Kent. Just finishing the last hole. Should be fine now. No chance of someone trippin' in 'em and hurting themselves."

"Good to hear. Brought your guest for ya."

This time his head snapped up and around, and he totally focused on the two of us. "Ari. Glad you could make it." He offered a beaming smile.

"Y'all have a nice ride," Kent said. He tipped his hat to me. "Ari. Pleasure."

As Kent walked off, Gavin made a move toward me, then apparently reconsidered. "Let me duck into the washroom and get cleaned up some. Then I'll give you a proper greeting."

The moment he returned, properly dressed in a short-sleeved paisley shirt, jeans, and his hat, he swept me up into his arms, twirled me around, and placed a long kiss on my cheek as he set me down. "Thanks for coming out this way. Come. Let's go to the corral and get our mounts. I asked another wrangler to saddle a couple for us and have them ready for when you arrived." He grasped my hand and led me over to the stables and ring.

A group of pre-teen girls with a handful of adults hung around saddled horses, listening to a trail guide go over what the next couple of hours would entail. Nearby one of the younger females of the group seemed to be apprehensive of the activity and the horse beside her.

"Mind giving me a moment?" Gavin asked.

"No. Do what you have to do."

He went over to the woman and child, speaking with the adult for a bit before he hunkered down and spoke with the girl.

I could only catch a few words here and there, and from them, I gathered Gavin was helping her get over her fear of getting up on the horse. After a few more words, he lifted her up and put her in the saddle. The girl smiled. He spoke with the woman a little more, then jogged back over.

"Poor thing," Gavin said as he directed us into the building. "She wants to ride. She doesn't want to be left behind. Last time she went riding, though, she had a difficult animal, so she's spooked. I assured her and her mother she'd be all right on the trail. She's riding the ranch's most docile mount, and Dakota, the wrangler leading the scout troop, is one of the best ranch hands around."

Adoring how he had a way of putting people at ease and making them feel special, I sighed. His kindness was refreshing.

Gavin showed me to a horse by the name of Ebony, a mare whose color matched my hair. "She shouldn't give you much trouble," he stated, patting her hind end. He grabbed her reins and gave them to me. Then he went to another horse and started to lead him out of the stables with me following behind. "We're going to set off for one of the easier trails. Figured if you haven't ridden in a while, it'll get you used to the saddle again and give me a chance to gage your competence level before we tackle one of the more difficult paths."

"Sounds fair to me."

We mounted our horses and set out. As he took the lead, I admired the sight before me—strong back, nice ass—and it wasn't the horse I was looking at. Gavin had such a good seat on the horse and seemed to fit in so naturally on the ranch, I couldn't imagine him doing anything else with his life. He seemed made for the life of a wrangler.

Gavin glanced over his shoulder. "We're gonna jog up to the top of Sunset Hill. Come on." He spurred his mount into a slightly faster gate.

Ebony followed at the same pace without much prompting from me, and within several minutes, we found ourselves at the top of a hill overlooking some of the property. A small cabin with the same stone façade sat nestled behind a few trees. A weathered wood sign reading *Dove's Nest* pointed in its direction. Nearby stood a canopy porch swing bed, a fire pit, and a picnic table.

"Area's used for romantic getaways, but when the cabin's not booked, people come up here to watch the sunsets."

"Hence the name," I added.

Gavin bobbed his head, leaned forward, and rested his arms on the pommel of his saddle. He gazed out over the land.

"Penny for your thoughts?" I asked, wondering what had made him become pensive.

"Sometimes I miss California. But when it comes down to it, I am glad I'm back. Glad we've reconnected. I remember how Sis and I enjoyed you as our sitter. You were much more 'lenient' than others we'd had."

Considering I still felt odd about the age difference and that aspect of our lives, I attempted to change the subject. "You told me you worked on a ranch out west and became interested in the search and rescue organization, but did you have a chance to go to college at all? Have any kind of serious relationship?"

"I had girlfriends, but nothing serious. No one I really wanted to bring home to meet the family. As for college, I got my associate degree. Took some higher courses in psychology and criminal justice, but I got so busy with work and SAR that pursuing a higher degree took a backseat."

"Criminal justice, you say?"

He nodded again. "Had some thoughts of becoming a cop, or going into the FBI, or something."

"Interesting," was all I dared say, feeling that if we continued along the lines of the conversation, we'd end up talking about Chad. I also decided against mentioning it might not have been the mob shows that had piqued his interest about my stalker ex-boyfriend.

Chadwick. That obsessive and possessive prick. He'd called three times and texted twice trying to reach me before I'd left for the ranch. I'd ignored it all. Breathing in the cleansing, crisp air, I turned my face up toward the bright sun and deep blue sky. At least out here I didn't have a signal and could have some peace. Not that I had my phone with me. I'd left it in my car for fear of losing it in the wilderness.

"Yeah." He sat up. "Let's continue on."

He led us down the other side of the hill. We meandered on trails around the property keeping the conversation light and superficial—about the weather, a couple of movies we wanted to see, some current events in the news—which was totally fine with me. I just wanted to enjoy the day, the ease of it, and being with someone who didn't hold me to extreme standards and didn't want anything from me.

Smiling, I stole a quick glance at Gavin. He looked so comfortable and self-assured. Yet his poise didn't come off as arrogant like Chad's. No. Gavin seemed quite different. He happened to be a kind and thoughtful man, as respectful, if not more, than his parents had been. It warmed my heart the way he'd helped that young girl and how well he treated the animals.

All too soon the trail looped back to the ranch. Out in the ring, we dismounted, then walked the horses around to cool them down. Gavin removed their gear, brushed them, and we led them into the stables to their individual stalls.

As Gavin made sure they were secured behind the gates with plenty of water and some hay and feed, I strolled down the center walkway. Two horses had been left behind from the morning's rides, but they didn't seem too upset. I cooed at them as I passed by. When I arrived at the end, I peeked down the left row and the right one, taking in all the tack and saddles hanging on the wall and lining the workbenches on either side of a few doorways.

"Ari? You okay?"

"Yes, just being nosy," I replied and turned to head back over to Gavin, who happened to be leaning up against one of the empty stalls next to the horse, Ebony, I'd ridden. He'd hooked his thumbs into the belt loops of his jeans and had one booted foot up against the door. The tilt of his head and hat cast shadows, nicely shading the angles and planes of his face. Dust from the trail coated his boots and some of his clothes.

Perfectly rugged and sexy.

The artist in me wished I'd brought sketching materials along so I could capture the moment. Or better yet have kept my phone on me. I could have snapped a picture and then painted him later in the privacy of my own space where I could let my fantasies flow free.

A slight movement on his part revealed his eyes. The intense, direct stare of his gaze made me question my decision to roam the building. Unsure of the nearby exits, I glanced away from him and closed my eyes.

I had to fight the panic sprouting within me. Ever since childhood, when my friends and I almost couldn't escape a theater during an emergency, not knowing escape routes tended to give me anxiety. Chad hadn't helped either. When his treatment grew rougher, I always tried to make sure I had a way to leave. Not knowing if a doorway leading to the outside was behind me or not made me antsy.

Gavin's not that lying cheater Chad. Gavin wouldn't hurt me.

But did I really know that for sure?

Slowly, I turned my head and opened my eyes. An empty stall containing what looked to be fresh hay sitting in a pile in the back corner caught my attention. The ground appeared to have been cleaned.

Fighting the urge to run, I looked back at him.

His gaze had grown passionate, and his lips had curled into a rakish smile.

My heart fluttered. My knees went weak. The atmosphere seemed electrified.

Any hints of anxiety were swept away due to the sensual magnetism pulsating between us, and all my thoughts fled. Save for one.

What would it be like to have a roll in the hay?

Being sexually adventurous had never been a strong suit. Much to the chagrin of Chad and a couple other ex-boyfriends. Yet, the thought of trying new places and positions with Gavin didn't quite fill me with the Catholic school girl guilt and shame the nuns and my *abuela* had instilled in me as a youngster. Heat crept into my cheeks.

Gavin took a few steps toward me. His grin widened. "Your cheeks have turned a lovely shade of pink. What is going through that pretty head of yours?"

His voice had deepened, and the words rolled so flirtatiously off his tongue, I had to swallow to clear my throat and find my voice. "Um..." I stammered with another glance at the pile. "The hay."

"The hay, huh?"

He drew closer, and this time I did step away. Right into the outer wall of a stall next to the clean one. Seemingly, right where he wanted me.

Gavin placed his hands on either side of me, essentially locking me into place. I nodded in answer, hoping that'd be the end of the conversation. But then, my mouth decided to have different plans. What I'd been thinking tumbled out. "I saw the fresh straw and couldn't help wondering what it'd be like to make love in it."

"Not very comfortable."

His quick, deadpan reply stunned me. "Oh." My heart fell. A silly reaction considering we barely knew each other, but I'd been expecting a different response. I realized I'd kind of hoped it'd be something he and I could have experienced together, perhaps for the first time for both of us. Then again, of course he'd know about the hay. He'd worked around ranches for ages. He'd had a life before he *re*-met me.

"Yeah, one afternoon I found a stall much like this and thought it'd be a good place to hunker down in and catch a quick nap. I'd been on duty the night before, and my ass had been draggin' all morning." He gave a slight shake of his head. "The hay I'd been on got hard as it compressed. It poked and scratched something fierce. Got to the point where I'd thought I'd have better luck sleepin' on a porcupine."

Poking. Scratching. I knew how I wanted to be poked and scratched.

Having a difficult time keeping my naughty thoughts to a minimum, I focused on the top button of his shirt since it was close to eye level. "Duty?"

"Huh? Oh, um, SAR. It was my night to volunteer."

"Right. Well, thanks for the heads up about the hay. Good to know."

"Next time I do something like that. Or anything else," he added, cupping my chin, tilting my head up, and winking. "I'll have a blanket with me. I almost have a mind to go find one right now, so we could put it to the test, but I am on the clock. It's our first date anyway. Something like foolin' around in the hay would be better once we got more acquainted. Right?"

"Yes, I suppose so." Everything inside me hummed. His nearness was bewitching, and how could a man who worked around horses all day smell so good?

Hill country air. Leather.

Man.

Any anxiousness I'd felt about being trapped had washed away in the surge of longing for the cowboy. Primal, womanly instincts gripped me, urged me to kiss the pulsing spot in his neck, trail my tongue down to the dip where his shoulder and torso met, rest my hands on his chest and feel the beat of his heart and his strength.

God, I wanted to kiss him, and not that chaste kind we'd exchanged in the coffee shop. No, I wanted something like I'd seen in the movies, a soul searing lip lock that could only be experienced by two people destined for each other.

Gavin's heated gaze bore into mine. "Doesn't mean I can't do this, though."

As if he'd read my mind, he gave me exactly what I'd wanted.

He lowered his mouth, claimed mine with unrestrained intensity, and my knees almost gave way. Lips tingling from the contact, I melted into the kiss. No longer did I have the desire to flee, to escape from the building and from him. As he wrapped me in his arms, I pressed my mouth firmer onto his and slipped my arms around his waist. Happiness filled me, and for the first time in months, I felt safe, like I'd been reunited with a part of my soul that'd broken away due to Chad's abuse.

Gavin's tongue breached my lips and joined with mine in a dance of reckless abandon. Overloaded with sensation from his touches, a small moan escaped me, and my unfettered reaction chiseled away the dam to my logic and libido. Any qualms I'd had about him—us—vanished. I brought my hands around to the front of his jeans and started fumbling with his belt.

Right as he deepened the kiss, a cough behind Gavin broke the magic we'd been weaving.

"Sorry to interrupt," Kent said, "but, Gavin, we need you out in the ring. A group's come back early."

Without looking back at the man, Gavin replied, "Be there in a sec, Kent." Then to me he said, "I guess this ends our first date. I know it wasn't much, but I'll make it up to you soon. See you tomorrow in class, yeah?"

"Yes, of course," I stated on a whispered breath, slightly embarrassed we'd been caught like a couple of teens making out in a basement and all heady with desire.

"Good."

He kissed the top of my head, released me, and hurried off.

I made quick work getting back to my vehicle. There was no way I wanted to run into Kent and be reminded of how we'd been an exhibit for his viewing pleasure.

A few hours later, after a couple of stops to do errands, I stood before my easel, blank canvas staring at me. I wanted to paint Gavin as I'd seen him in the barn, but the first strokes of the portrait weren't coming to me for some reason.

Was this how writer's felt facing a blank screen with a pure white page? A flashing cursor seeming to mock the scribe, saying—type something, type something—while said scribe had no idea what the first line would be? In my case, the white gessoed canvas taunted me, and the brush felt like a lead weight.

Deciding to refocus on something easier to get my hand moving, I changed the orientation of the canvas and squeezed some yellow oxide onto my palette. A wash of the color as an underpainting would do well for the desert sunset landscape I had in mind.

The last of the stretched white cloth faded away to a golden-like hue, and as I rinsed my brush in the jar of water, my cell phone rang. Hoping it'd be Gavin, I hurried over to the other side of the room where it sat on its charger a safe distance away from my acrylics.

Chadwick.

This time I took the call, not bothering to say hello. "Chad, you have to stop harassing me."

"Where the hell have you been? I've been trying to reach you for hours! Why don't you answer your God damned cell?"

I held the phone away from my head to protect my eardrum from his barking. When he was done spewing choice curse words my way, I replied, "Because I don't have to answer to you anymore. I don't have to pick up the phone when you call. The only reason I hit 'accept' this time was to tell you to stop. Stop. Calling. Me. Stop harassing me. We. Are.

Over. We aren't a couple. We've been over for months. Over, Chadwick. If you don't understand what I mean, look up the words in the dictionary. If you persist in trying to talk to me or see me, I will have no recourse but to take legal action."

"Bitch! Fu—"

Before he could finish, I disconnected the call. My body shook uncontrollably. Anger over his words, his past treatment of me, and how I still let him get to me, combined with the stark, fearful realization that in his crazed mood he could come after me. Then there was the shame. I hadn't been smart enough to recognize the signs of a bad relationship until it was too late. I'd been in love and invested my trust. I'd been a fool, believing he was *the one. My person.*

All the mixed emotions wound together into a tight coil. Then as I put down my phone, they sprang with a surprising force of energy, causing a physiological reaction so strong it almost brought me to my knees.

That man chilled and disturbed me to my core more than I cared to admit.

I went to my kitchen pantry, pulled out a bottle, and poured myself a three-finger full tumbler of my "for special occasions" extra-aged tequila. After a couple of swigs, I refilled the glass then carried it to the master bathroom. I'd shower, drink, and afterward, I'd take a long nap in which I hoped to dream of Gavin and the day we shared, praying by doing so, it would chase away the misery Chad had thrust into my life.

CHAPTER FOUR

After I'd sufficiently calmed myself the night before, was able to work on the abstract sunset, and refocus my thoughts on Gavin, anticipation of seeing him in class and what the day would bring shooed away any lingering dark clouds hanging over my head.

Had I been that brazen at the ranch to bring up getting it on in the hay? Yes. Had he said no? No.

If Kent hadn't interrupted us, what would Gavin and I have gotten up to? Would we have spent our first time together in a barn?

Quite possible.

The idea warmed me yet spooked me.

As much as I didn't want to grow old alone, after my experience with Chad I'd been leery about getting into a new relationship. I thanked God Chad and I never tied the knot. If I thought things were bad now? Imagine a divorce with that asshole. That would have been a nightmare.

Taking a deep breath to clear my head, I hurried into the arts building and up the stairs, picturing Gavin standing as he had in the stable. The image sent my stomach fluttering. I couldn't remember the last time I was excited to see someone. Screw Chad and my non-desire to find a relationship. With Gavin around, there was the potential for me to love again. Maybe even hear wedding bells at some distant point in the future.

The hall near my office happened to be devoid of people. For once, I'd arrived at the university with lots of extra time to spare. I rounded the corner, and a man stepped into my path.

"Hello, Arianna. I'm going to ask you again. Where have you been? You weren't in the café this morning."

Tilting my head back, I looked up at Chad and had to fight the urge to spit in his face. "You are dense, aren't you." My voice came out so flat and with no inflection that what I'd said sounded more like a statement than a question. "You've left me no choice. I'm going to get a restraining order against you." I went to step around him.

"Right." Chad put his arm out and blocked my progress. "Sure. My girl wouldn't do that to me." He reached out toward my face.

I swatted his hand away then brushed a stray lock of hair behind my ear. "I am not your girl. Did you not hear a word I'd said on the phone yesterday?"

"You didn't mean any of that."

"Pardon?" I huffed in exasperation. "Yes. I did. Read my lips, Chad. We are over. Done. *Terminado.* And since you can't stop stalking me, showing up where you're not wanted, and keep attempting to engage me in conversation, I'll do what I should have done months ago. I'll go to the cops."

Chad's face turned crimson. "You'll do no such thing."

"You seem to keep forgetting we've broken up. I kicked you to the curb. I can do whatever the hell I want."

He shook his head.

"Don't you shake your head at me," I stated with force to overcome any trembling that I feared would come through my voice, "and don't you dare get mad at me. If anyone should be mad, it should be me. I wasn't the one shoving my tongue, and God knows what else, down other women's throats while we were together."

"Tracy meant nothing."

"Well, she must have meant something. That hadn't been the first time you'd been with her. Or with Jill. Or with Cindy. Or Brooke."

His eyes widened, and his mouth made a tiny O.

"Don't pretend to be shocked. I'd had a good idea you'd been cheating. But catching you with Tracy at the club was my confirmation. Like I'd said then, and I'll say again now, you, your tiny dick, and whore sluts can go to hell."

A muscle twitched along Chad's clenched jaw. The alarming look in his gaze had me backing away. I'd seen that expression before, and a backhand to the face usually followed. Shifting on my feet, I started to turn to run, but then it seemed as if time warped, and everything around me moved in slow motion. Chad raised his arm again, crossed it in front of his body, and wound up for a knuckle slap.

Before I could move, the back of his hand hit my face. My skin stung where he'd made contact. Dazed, I gingerly touched the spot, then cursed the fact that there'd be a mark.

He pointed at me. "Don't ever speak to me like that again. And that guy you're screwing? Stay away from him. He's not doing me or my business any good."

Tears welled in my eyes, not just from the pain but from the shame of being weak, of not being able to defend myself against Chad because I didn't know how to fight back. So many times, I'd told myself to take self-defense classes, but I'd never book the course, thinking Chad would keep to his word and change. Then after we broke up, I didn't think I'd need them. I should have at least learned how to throw a return punch.

And how did he know I was seeing someone? Was he having me followed? Was he stalking me more than I'd thought?

Not only all that, but what the hell was he talking about regarding his *business*?

I must have said the last word out loud, or he'd seen the question in my gaze, because he answered, "Never you mind. Stay away from him. Keep to yourself. Better yet, you and I are going out on a date. This Saturday. I'll pick you up at seven." He grabbed my chin and squeezed. "You won't stand me up if you know what's good for you." Forcefully, he released me and pushed at the same time.

My ankle twisted. I crashed to the floor.

A sadistic grin spread Chad's lips, and his gaze grew wild, as if excited I'd ended up in a submissive position. He balled his hand and brought his arm back, pointing his fist in my direction.

Blocked in by him and the wall, I had no chance of rising and escaping before he could land a punch. I squeezed my eyes shut, not wanting to watch the blow that was no doubt heading my way.

Too bad I was so early that no one roamed the halls. I could have used a witness. For someone to see Chadwick's abuse, it'd make for an easier time of pressing charges and putting him in jail. But as it stood now, the whole thing would be a he-said-she-said situation, and with his charm and connections, he'd probably get off scot-free.

"Hey! You! Leave her alone."

I peeked out one eye and looked around Chad's leg. The stranger's voice belonged to a gorgeous, dark-haired man I didn't recognize. At first, I thought it might be a student, but he was with Gavin and wearing a suit jacket. They ran toward us.

Chad pointed at me again. "This isn't over. See you Saturday," he stated and took off before the stranger and Gavin could get to him.

"Ari?" Gavin rushed up and squatted beside me. "You all right?"

"Yes. I am now that you're here." I took a calming breath. "And I'll be even better once I get a restraining order against Chad. Maybe take some self-defense classes, too."

"Yeah, I agree. You need an order. I'll help you with some moves, too." Gavin rose, clenched his fists, and glared in the direction Chad went. "Fucking asshole. I'm gonna kill that bastard for putting his hands on you like that. In fact—"

Gavin's expression darkened. His gaze turned wild. Veins popped out along his temples. He stepped around me and pushed by the guy he was with, acting like he was about to chase after Chad.

"Bishop." Gavin's companion grabbed his arm. The man's fingers turned white from the effort of restraining Gavin. "No," he said with a stern tone and shook his head. "I get you want to give the prick a piece of your mind and take him down a peg or two, but this really needs to be handled on a legal level. Get me?"

Gavin jerked a thumb at some imaginary point down the hall. "For fuck's sake, Russo, he—"

"I know, man, but there's nothing you can do right now." Russo released Gavin and glanced down at me with an outstretched hand. "Can you stand?"

Nodding, I allowed him to help me to my feet. "Aside from my face, only my pride's been injured."

"Becoming a protected person seems like a good idea," the stranger said. "If you need any help with it, let me know."

I raised a brow and looked at Gavin.

Appearing to gather himself, Gavin breathed deep. The muscles in his face and neck relaxed. The enraged cast to his eyes and savage expression disappeared. "Arianna, this is Detective Zachary Russo. He's a buddy of mine from California. Met him through SAR. Then he moved to Vegas and joined Metro there. He came out for a surprise visit."

"A cop?"

Gavin bobbed his head. "He wanted to see what I've been up to here, and after I told him about you, he wanted to meet the woman I've been spending time with."

"Okay." A part of me felt flattered that Gavin had been chatting me up, but I couldn't get my focus off the fact Zachary was a cop. Looking at Gavin's friend, I asked, "You see Chad hit me?"

Zachary shook his head. "Saw you fall and him attempt to punch you, but from the discoloration forming across your cheekbone, it's no secret he's the one who caused it."

"Good." I released a breath. "Finally. A witness."

"Two witnesses," Gavin added, sidling up to me and wrapping an arm around my waist. "Maybe you should cancel class today."

I didn't have words to describe how happy I was he was there, that he'd wanted to go after Chad, and how relieved I was he looked himself again and not like an angry caveman, but telling me to not work? I wasn't having any of that. "Can't. It'll set back projects."

"But you've just—"

Turning out of Gavin's hold, I held up a hand, stopping his protest. "I know what I've gone through, and I appreciate your concern, but I have obligations. I can't let Chad believe he's gotten the better of me. I also think some of the students would be disappointed if they couldn't 'see' you today."

Zachary chuckled. "And I'm sure Bishop loves every minute of the modeling."

Gavin's worried look morphed to surprise, as if he'd been caught doing something naughty. Pink blossomed on his face and streaked down his neck.

"I think that's my cue to go," Zachary said. "Thanks, Bishop, for showing me around. I'll see you when you're done here."

Skin color returning to normal, Gavin offered a weak smile. "No problem, Russo."

Still chuckling, Zachary smacked Gavin on the back then walked away.

Gavin shot him a glare, then focused back on me. "We need to get some ice on your cheeks. Is there a break room or something nearby where we can get some?"

"Around the corner and down the hall."

"Great. Let's cool down that mark on your face and get class over with so we can get you home."

* * * *

"I can't believe how open you were. That you were truthful when the students asked you about your face."

I shoved the key into the lock of the interior garage door. "Why should I lie about how my ex got handsy? They're adults. They should see what cruelty and disrespect does. And yes, before you ask again, I am going to get a protective order."

"That's not what I was going to ask. What I want to know is why you lock the door here? People shouldn't be able to get into your garage when it's closed."

"I've learned I can't be too careful when it comes to Chad. I have a security screen door out front that's double locked as is my solid front door. My front and side windows are blocked so light can't be seen outside. This way he can't tell if I'm home or not. At least here I feel safe. Thought I was safe at work, too." I touched my cheek that still throbbed then pushed the door open. "Now I'm not sure about anything."

"You can be sure that as long as we're together, I'll do my best to make sure nothing happens to you. Now, go sit. I'll get you some more ice. You want a glass of water or anything?"

I glanced over my shoulder as he locked the door. "I think my cheek's okay. What I need is something stronger. In the pantry on the top shelf is a bottle of extra-aged tequila. Glasses are in the cabinet over the sink. Make it three fingers tall." In the living room, I sat on the couch and did something I normally hated doing—I put my feet up on the coffee table.

"Want ice or water in it?"

"*Dios mío*, no. Straight up is the only way I'll drink it."

"Mind if I have some?"

"Have at it."

Moments later, Gavin brought in two tumblers of the amber liquid and handed me one, along with a package of frozen peas.

"Thanks. Oh, and keep in mind, it's a sipping drink. Not the kind you shoot." I held the bag of vegetables to my cheek.

"Got it." He took a taste. "Wow. This is smooth."

"It's my 'for special times' drink, but considering the phone call last night and then what happened earlier, I'm making it my 'forget about Chad' drink." Used to the alcohol's taste, I took a large mouthful.

"Phone call? Mind telling me exactly what's gone on?"

I put down the peas, filled him in on the call, how Chad had found me in the hall, and what we'd discussed. "I don't know what he meant about you ruining his business. How can a wrangler ruin a hotel concierge? I don't even know how he knew I'd started seeing you."

Gavin shrugged. "Got me."

"I'm so glad you showed up when you did."

"So am I." He put his arm around me and gave my shoulders a squeeze. "I'm serious when I'd said that I'll do what's in my power to keep you safe."

"I appreciate that."

His face drew near to mine as if leaning in for a kiss. Anticipation coiled within me. But then he tilted his head and planted his lips on my forehead. Disappointment shoved the eagerness aside.

He stood. "I should get going. Let you rest."

I didn't like the pit forming in my stomach with the thought of him leaving and me being alone. It almost felt like I was being abandoned. Reaching out, I grasped his hand. "Don't go. I'd like you to stay. That is, if you don't have somewhere you need to be."

"Nope. The rest of my day and evening are open."

"Good." I yanked on his hand to bring him back down onto the couch, and I planted my lips on his.

Gavin kissed me in return, but all too soon he pulled away. "Ari, I'm not sure this is a good idea. I don't want to be an emotional crutch, a rebound guy, or a tool in some kind of revenge maneuver. If we're going to be together, I don't want it to be in Chad's shadow."

Shifting and looking straight ahead, I sighed. "I understand, but really, I had...have...none of that in mind. My attraction to you is solely based on—" A knock at my front door interrupted my little speech. "*Mierda*. Talk about bad timing."

"I'll go see who it is and get rid of them, if you want?"

"Please."

I watched him walk across the room into the small foyer and open the door, leaving the security screen door closed and locked. The voices were muffled until one boomed and seemed to project into the house.

"I don't know who the fuck you think you are, but you're going to let me in now," Chad yelled. "I want to see my girl. I want to see Arianna."

"¡*Maldita sea!*," I muttered. *Chad*.

I rose and hurried to the front door. Standing to the side and slightly behind Gavin, I put my hands on my hips. "Chad, go away. You're not welcome here anymore." Though I couldn't see Chad very well through the metal screen, I knew his face was probably turning crimson again.

"I thought I told you to stay away from this jerk."

Taking a deep breath, I counted to ten, so I could state in the calmest, clearest voice I could, "That's the thing, Chad, we're not together, and you're not listening. I'm going to sound like a broken record here, but maybe this time my words will get through that thick skull of yours. One, we're not a couple. Two, I don't have to listen to you, which means, three, I can be friends with, and date, whomever I want. Four, like I said, you're not welcome here. I'll be obtaining a restraining order on you. If you try to do anything to impede it, it won't work. I have witnesses to your abuse. Now, go. Leave me alone and never darken my doorstep again." I turned to head back to the couch.

Behind me, Gavin added, "You heard the lady. Get lost." He slammed the door.

Outside, Chad yelled some curse words, banged on the door, then a minute later a car revved and sped off.

Gavin was at my side, enveloping me in his arms. "That guy is something. If I wasn't—" He cut himself off and took a deep breath. "If I didn't know better, I'd have barged outside and given him a dose of my fists. I'm going to ask you again, are you sure he's not into something?"

"If you're talking about the illegal business stuff, I have no idea. All I know is what I've already told you."

Gavin sighed. "Don't hate me for what I'm about to say, but I have a hard time believing you didn't know what he was up to at work or when he was doing his club thing."

Wincing, I fought flinching away from him. After all, he did have a point, but I had been stupidly naïve. "He wasn't always like this. Our relationship had been great for a while. Open. Communicative. Then he stopped telling me about his day. He never kept work files here. Never wrote in a journal. His phone was always with him. Not that I could figure out his passcode."

"So, you did try to find out what he'd been up to?"

I disliked acknowledging how I'd been the paranoid girlfriend, suspicious about his excuses and his whereabouts, and had tried to find out what was going on a personal level. "Yes. I did. But not because of his work. I hated prying, but if I hadn't snooped, I wouldn't have confirmed his lies and cheating." I shifted again and caught his gaze. "What's with the questions?"

"Remember at the café how I'd said there might be something more going on with Chad. Hearing his voice through the screen and seeing bits and pieces of him, I sensed something was off. I wonder if he's using."

"Using? As in drugs?" A slight chill streaked through me. Why hadn't I thought about that? Maybe I could have gotten him some help.

"Yeah. It's a possibility. I guess he never mentioned getting high or anything?"

"Far as I always knew, he hated taking drugs, at least prescriptions and over the counter products. He'd rather suffer with a headache, he'd say, than put the chemicals in his body." But was it another lie? "Look, can we stop talking about Chad?" Dealing with my ex was taxing, and I was tired of it all. I sank back into Gavin's embrace. "God, I'm so glad you're here. Otherwise, he probably would've forced his way in. Who knows what would've happened then."

Especially if he is strung out on a narcotic.

"Yeah. Good thing I hadn't left." He kissed the top of my head. "Want to watch television or something?"

After Chad's unexpected visit and the somber conversation, I couldn't stand the thought of sitting and staring at a box. I needed to lighten the mood. Be creative. Since I had the perfect subject matter at my disposal, I came up with an idea. "Actually, I'd love to paint you."

"Paint me?"

The surprise in his voice made me giggle. I sat up and looked at him. "I don't get a chance to do much in class with overseeing the students, but I've been wanting to make some artwork featuring you ever since you appeared in my art class."

Gavin appeared to think about my suggestion, then shrugged and lifted the corner of his mouth. "I'm up for it if you are, *Special Lady*."

The meaning behind his words wasn't lost on me, but I pretended to ignore it. "Wonderful. Painting always helps clear my head and makes me feel better. Let's go into my studio."

"You have a studio here?"

"One of the bedrooms. Nothing fancy. But it's set up so I can make a mess and not worry about it."

I led him into my creative space, reflecting to him how I'd hoped that by this time in my life, I would have made more of a name for myself and been sponsored with a studio down in Southtown. But big studio or not, at least I had a job doing what I loved, a roof over my head, food in the fridge, and I could do what I wanted with my art. No art publisher was looking over my shoulder telling me what I could or couldn't do either.

"It can suck having to adhere to strict rules and schedules." Gavin followed me into the room. "Sometimes I'm jealous of those who can throw out the playbook and work outside the box. Then again, not like I have a normal nine to five, and my desk is the great outdoors. So, what did you have in mind?"

A cowboy hat rested on the table. I'd picked it up on the way home from Gateway on the off chance I'd get him to sit for me.

"Put on that cowboy hat and unbutton your shirt."

CHAPTER FIVE

"Yes, ma'am." Gavin seemed more than pleased to do as I asked and started to undo the fastenings of his shirt. "Whatever you need."

I directed him to stand next to the window facing my backyard. The warm, golden glow of afternoon light streamed in through the glass in such a way that I felt I could recreate part of the scene from the stables. Once I had Gavin in position—dipped head, fingers gracing the brim of the hat, booted foot planted against the wall—I noticed how the illumination highlighted part of him and cast shadows in the right spots. "Great. Hold it there." I picked up my sketching materials, sat, and set to work.

"I thought you wanted to paint me."

"Not yet."

God, he's sexy as hell, I thought as I mapped an outline of his form. My hand trembled slightly, and I wondered if I'd be able to do the piece justice with how my hormones were getting the best of me. He'd come to my defense, seemed to care for me, and was interested in being my art subject. That alone was enough to endear him to me, but his bedroom-eyed gaze peered at me from beneath the hat so invitingly, a hot, sweeping tug at my pussy made me lose my focus for a moment. I squirmed in my seat trying to find relief.

When the fine line I'd tried to pencil onto the paper looked more like a squiggle, I decided to change tactics. "Hold on a sec, Gavin." I ran out to the living room, grabbed my phone, and hurried back, snapping several pictures upon my return.

"I'm okay in this position if you need more time to draw."

"It's not that." I checked the images to make sure they weren't blurred.

"Okay, but if artists use photos, why have a model pose at all?"

"Huh?" Perplexed, I raised a brow and stared at him, then remembered—he's a wrangler, not an art student. My world was different than his. Where I got messy with colors, he was used to dust on his boots, the heat and dirt of the land and animals, sweat on his brow and chest...

Picturing him on the ranch, shirtless and sweaty under the hot Texas sun, working with his hands, sent another warm rush of pleasure through me.

Before my imagination could run away and make my mouth say things better left in my head, like, "Why would I want to use photos of a gorgeous man when I could have the real thing?", I put on my proverbial professor's hat. "You're right. It seems odd to pose when photos can be used, but the pictures have their place. They can be used as references for fine detail and finishing work after the model has gone. But having the model present, a 3D version, is super beneficial. It can lend a certain atmosphere to the piece. Invoke emotional responses in the artist that will come through to the art. Plus, being able to get up and look at the subject matter from a different angle in real time helps, too. Seeing how light plays with the planes and angles and contours, and how it changes as time ticks by. Sometimes those subtle nuances add to the piece, and the distinctions can get lost in a photograph. Especially through the lens of an inexperienced photographer."

Plus, now I have something to look at when you're not around.

"Got it."

Smiling, I studied him some more. Every time I looked at his chiseled chest and the strip of hair going in a line from his belly button to a spot hidden by his jeans, my heart fluttered. Sure, I'd seen a lot of him in class, but this was just the two of us.

This was intimate.

I wanted to run my fingers along his skin. Play with the patch of hair. See where my caresses would lead to. I wanted to *create* with him. I'd felt this way with other boyfriends, even Chad, but never had the urge been so strong. Nor had I been able to gather the courage to do anything about it in the past. Except once. When my relationship with Chad had started imploding, a friend of mine gave me an art kit, one designed to help couples grow closer to each other. I'd shown it to Chad. He'd then called the gift, my idea, and me stupid, telling me I must be an idiot to think he'd be interested in such a "childish, preposterous activity."

Asking him if he thought my career were those things, as well, spurred on a multi-hour argument that ended with him leaving and not returning for two nights. When he'd finally come home, he'd seemed remorseful and promised to do better by me. He had, too. For a couple of weeks. But we never had used the present.

Now would be a good time to make some new memories surrounding those art supplies.

After all, I seemed to have a very willing participant, who happened to be gorgeous in my opinion, beautifully proportioned in a trim, well-toned way, and *desired* little ol' *me*. Gavin wanted me, had admitted to dreaming and fantasizing about me. Despite my concerns about our ages and how we used to know each other, I realized I felt the same about him.

I hungered for him.

"God, I want to paint you," the awed words fell from my mouth before I could stop them.

"Thought that's what we're doing," Gavin responded.

Clearing my throat, I jerked my attention from him, went to my paints, and faked looking for one. "Well, yes, but…" *Spit it out, girl. Be brave. Have some fun.* Gathering my resolve, I continued, "I want to get out a gift a friend of mine had given me a while back. It contains non-toxic paints. This way I can *paint you.* Use you as both palette and canvas. And, if you're up for it, you can paint me."

An impish grin stretched his face. "Sounds interesting. What do we need to do?"

Swallowing hard, I watched him take a couple steps toward me. I couldn't believe my idea was coming to fruition. After the spiel he'd given me earlier and saying he should leave, I didn't think he'd agree so readily. "Well, the first thing we should do is get down to our undergarments."

"Wouldn't getting completely naked be better for something like this?"

Gavin's voice had been low, the seductive words rolled off his tongue and lapped at my ears in such a way it made me tingle. Heat bloomed throughout my body at the promise of what was to come. "Well… Yes. Um…" I'd imagined this going a little smoother, being more spontaneous, but the question and my physical response threw me off guard. My mind started churning over the process.

The kit I'd been given had four different paint colors, a canvas, a plastic tarp, booties for the feet, and a couple of other goodies to get lovers in the mood to paint while enjoying foreplay. But the mess. Paint in places I might not want. Sure, the pigments were specially formulated, but I didn't want to take the chance of getting a urinary tract infection or something worse down there.

"Ari?"

He appeared concerned, and I hated feeling like I was ruining the moment, especially when I *wanted* him. Not just because it'd been months since I'd had sex, but because I felt an energetic attachment to him. I needed to feel it as a tangible connection as well.

"Sorry. I was thinking maybe we should move into my bathroom. Be easier to contain the paint and for us to clean up afterwards. As for being naked…" Were these words really coming out of my mouth?

"Even though the paints are organic, I'd still be concerned about it getting into sensitive areas."

"Fair enough. What can I help carry into the bathroom?"

From a cabinet, I pulled out an unopened paper tarp and handed it to him, then I grabbed the kit and led the way into my bedroom and the master bathroom. "Could you open that and help me spread it out?"

Once the floor, some of the tub, and the bottoms of the cabinets were covered by the protection, I sat and tore into the box of supplies. As I laid out the plastic, the canvas, and lined up the paints, Gavin shucked his shirt, followed by his boots, jeans, and socks. He picked up the book of love poems, glanced through it, and then plucked the instructions from where I'd laid them on the floor.

"Okay, so you've done step one already," he read. "Says here we're supposed to put the paint on the canvas and then use our bodies."

I looked up from the supplies, trying to focus on his face and not the bulge cradled in his boxer briefs. "A man who reads directions?"

"What can I say? I'm a stickler for details. What color should we start with on the canvas?" he asked, taking a seat next to me.

His arm lightly brushed up against mine, feather-like, but electrifying. I tried to block his presence, the warmth radiating from him, for a moment. *Art. We're supposed to be creating a painting to represent the beginning of our relationship.* At least that's the way I was looking at the endeavor. "I'm thinking dark blue as part of the background."

"Like darkness. Like how I'd felt thinking I'd never see you again." Gavin picked up the small bottle of the dark liquid, opened it, and made a few squiggly lines on the canvas. He then settled onto his side on one half of it. "How my life seemed vast and empty until recently. Come." He patted a spot. "Join me."

You can't back out now, I silently told myself and stood. After removing my outfit and tossing my clothes and his on top of the counter, I joined him on the floor, facing him. As I adjusted my body to reflect his pose, elbow bent with my elevated head resting on my hand, the paint slid and squished beneath me. Cool to the touch. Tantalizing. I didn't care that I was ruining one of my better bra and panties. At least I wasn't in my wash-day granny items.

Gavin stared at me, his deep ocean-blue-eyed gaze boring into mine. Was he looking at me with admiration? Or was he wondering how to escape a potential coyote ugly situation? I wasn't young and svelte as I used to be. All at once I felt giddy but apprehensive. "Is everything okay?"

"Yeah," he replied in a soft voice. "I'm just appreciating your beauty and grateful I'm here. I can't believe anyone would treat you poorly or let you, a gem of a woman, get away." He brushed a lock of hair out of my face and cupped my cheek. Light and quick, he kissed me. "I have some ideas for the rest of the painting."

Such tender words. Such gentle caresses. I'd almost forgotten what it was like to be romanced, to have passion leisurely yet deliberately stoked instead of it being doused with lighter fluid and lit with a match. The fact that he, too, looked at this project as a reflection of our relationship, made my heart do cartwheels. "Great. What are you envisioning?" I asked in an equally quiet voice.

"I think white should go on next. Illumination in the darkness." Gavin maneuvered around to get the paint. After he faced me again and opened the container, he drizzled some onto my back. "Now that we've reconnected, I can't imagine going more than a couple of days without seeing you and your smile, hearing your voice and laughter. You brighten up my life, Arianna. You're my beacon."

Before I could react, he pulled me into his arms, swept me under him, and crushed his mouth upon mine. Beneath me and on me, the paint smeared. His hot body covered me like a weighted comforter, but not in an uncomfortable way, as his tongue swept into my mouth. The smooth sensation of his skin on mine, his contained strength, and the evidence of his arousal pressing against me, made me feel secure.

I could have stayed like this and kissed him forever.

But he seemed to have other thoughts in mind. Gavin lifted his head. "Think it's time for the red?" He grinned. "A passionate color." He kissed a cheek. "A powerful one." He kissed my other cheek, careful not to press on the bruise. "Like the love I feel for you growing within me."

Stunned by his poetic words, I couldn't nod, reply, or barely think. All I could do was gaze into his eyes.

"And, I tell ya, if I ever run across Chad again, I probably won't be able to keep my wits about me, and he will be introduced to my fists."

The thought of Gavin fighting for me stirred something fundamental in me. I'd never experienced a chivalrous man coming to my defense before and had come to believe being fought for only happened to other women. Now, I finally felt lucky, having landed a handsome, strong, renaissance man. Perhaps my karma was changing, and fate was being kind to me for once.

He tilted his head. "Ari? I didn't say something wrong, did I?"

Grinning, I shook my head. "No. Sorry. I was woolgathering."

"Ah. So, I was boring you."

"Not at all. I was reflecting on what you've been saying, and how I was feeling. For me to get lost in my head around you means I'm comfortable with you."

"I take it that's a good thing?"

"A very good thing. You do have a way with words, Mr. Bishop." My grin spread. "Grab me the red."

Gavin returned his own charming smile. "Guess I did learn something in all those humanities courses." He moved off me.

I took the opportunity to get to my feet, making sure to carefully peel the canvas off my back as I did so. "Stand up," I told him, taking the bottle out of his hand. "I want to try something."

The moment he was on his feet, I had him turn around. I applied some of the paint to my hand. "Looks like this is more orange than red. Oh, well. I'm going to put some of this on your butt. I'm hoping the underwear will give the artwork some interesting texture." After I coated his firm cheeks with the paint, I directed him to sit on the canvas.

Once he positioned himself on the floor again, I straddled him and sat on his lap. Our hands slick with paint rubbed up and down each other's backs as our lips came together. As we made out, I realized I wanted more than just embraces and kisses, and that no one was around to walk in on us this time. I pulled away. "I think we should get cleaned up."

He appeared a bit perplexed and released what sounded like a sigh of disappointment. "Yeah, guess you're right."

"Come on." After getting off him, I offered my hand.

Gavin took it and stood. The canvas stuck to his ass.

A giggle escaped me.

"I feel like a pin the tail on the animal novelty."

The giggle turned into a laugh as I tugged the sheet off him. On it, where he'd sat, looked to be a misshapen heart.

"That looks fitting," he said.

"Yes, it is." I placed the canvas back on the floor, turned and opened the curtain to the shower tub.

"What about the gold?"

After getting the faucet going, I sat on the edge, checked the water's temperature, and glanced up at him. "We'll worry about that later. For now…" I rose from my perch, reached behind me, unfastened my bra, then slipped out of my undergarments.

With what I hoped was a sexy, come hither look, I went into the tub and yanked up the tab for the shower. Warm water sluiced over my body. Color ran in rivulets down my skin. I dipped my head under the stream and slicked back my wet hair.

"You going to join me or not?" I asked, giving Gavin a flirty wink. The angel on my shoulder whispered how my grandmother would be worrying her rosary beads if she knew what I was doing. The vixen on my other shoulder told the goody two-shoes that *Abuela* wasn't here and wouldn't know.

Gavin made short work of removing his briefs and joining me in the shower. He pressed me up against the wall, and once again claimed my mouth. His kiss, full of passion, also demanded submission. My body turned into a live wire from the feel of his hot, slick skin rubbing along mine. My knees weakened.

He broke the kiss and put his lips near my ear. "I want you, Arianna, body, mind, soul. No matter what happens, I want you to know you're my priority. You've always been that and a part of my heart."

Despite the warm water washing over us, the wisp of his heated breath sent shivers down the side of my body. "I want you, too, Gavin."

Gavin nipped at my earlobe, kissed my neck below my ear, then did the same on the other side. He trailed the tips of his fingers across the top of my chest to my breasts. I gazed down at the hands working my mounds, and when he pinched the nipples, I sucked in a deep breath to keep from melting under his touch.

I closed my eyes. He stretched around me. A bottle clicked open. The pleasant scent of milk and honey filled the small area. Moments later, he soaped my torso, down to my butt cheeks. His strong fingers ran the lather along my legs, then my arms. Every line and curve of my body that he bathed smoldered with lust for him. Heady with desire, I opened my eyes and watched him cleanse himself all over, including his cock, which was as magnificent as I'd imagined it to be.

"Would you like me to help you with that?" I asked, keeping my gaze trained on his shaft and hoping he'd understand my meaning.

"Normally, I'd be happy for some hand and mouth play and say yes, but I'm already hard and ready for you." Gavin pulled down the handheld showerhead. He ran the water over me, then himself. "Spread your legs."

Doing what he requested created a little ball of need in my pussy, which was rewarded when he turned the stream toward the area. A moan of pleasure escaped my mouth. He chuckled then returned the shower head to its holder. When he turned back, he slipped his hand between my legs, fingered my slit, then slid his fingers into me.

"You're wet and ready for me, too," he said.

My whole being sank into blissful relaxation from his fondling. He massaged a breast, caressed my nether lips.

"I want to sink my cock into your moist heat. I want to be with you, Ari, never let you go." Gavin released my breast and slid his hand in tantalizing slowness along my abdomen to my hip while he removed his other hand from between my legs. He shifted, and in one easy movement, he braced me against the wall, with my legs wrapped around him, and had the head of his penis at my opening.

"I'm yours, Gavin. Take me."

In a swift motion, he pushed his length in. I moved my hips as best I could to meet his thrust and edge him in deeper. Waves of liquid fire coursed through me as his penis slid in and out of me in a rhythmic cadence. The shower beat down on us like a gentle rain, adding to the experience. He rotated his hips. Explosions of ecstasy went off in me with each of his strokes.

This was the connection I'd been seeking, the joining of two spirits, fulfilling destiny. I longed to be poetic like he'd been, profess words of adoration, and even though he'd mentioned love was growing in him, I wasn't sure if I was ready to admit mine out loud. Instead, I kissed him, trying through the intimate meeting of our mouths, to assure him of my feelings.

Soon, every nerve ending within me sparked and sizzled, and my muscles reeled with orgasmic contraction.

He broke the kiss and gripped me hard, nestling and moaning into the curve where my neck and shoulder met. I held onto him tightly, feeling his shudders. His breath quickened, and seconds later, he yanked himself out of me.

I felt the remains of his release on my thigh, and once my feet were on the floor of the tub again, he soaped down my lower torso and legs and rinsed me again. Then he turned off the water, swept me up in his arms, and carried me to bed.

We slept some and made love a couple more times. Gavin was poetic beauty in human male form and brooked no competition. And his cock! The bits and pieces only his *special lady* was able to see. To think I was her! Reflecting on its silky feel on my tongue as I'd pleasured him with my mouth once we moved to the bed, and then its hard warmth probing my core, made my body all tingly and hot again. I rolled over to snuggle up against him and found the other side of my bed empty.

Alarmed that he'd left and not said goodbye, I dressed and rushed out into the hall. The light in my studio was on.

"Gavin?" As I stepped into the room, he replaced a painting with the others leaning up against the wall.

"Sorry. Didn't mean to wake you. I'd wanted to look at these earlier." He waved a hand at the canvases. "They're wonderful. You really need to get them into a show. This way I can come and gush over them to other buyers and buy one myself. I could even have my friends swing by and make purchases."

"That'd be great. It's been a while since I've been in a show, or since I've been able to get down to the art district for a First Friday. My schedule is crazy now that I've taken over the additional classes. A show would be wonderful. What I'd really love to do is get gallery time at one of the high-end galleries."

Gavin picked up one of my favorite abstract landscape pieces, "Tide Pools at the Beach." The shades of blue, green, brown, and white were so calming. Part of me was glad I hadn't sold the piece yet.

"High-end like Luc and Neil Art Emporium?" At my questioning look, Gavin added, "Zach's a bit of an art collector. He talked about going to the district. Rattled off several names. That was one of 'em."

"Name sounds cheesy, doesn't it? I can see why it'd stick out in your mind. Name aside, it's actually an exclusive gallery. Chad once mentioned he might know somebody who might know someone to help me get in, but it never panned out."

Gavin's eyes darkened, and a probing query appeared to register in his hard gaze, but as quick as that happened, the puzzled, harsh expression disappeared. "That's too bad. You deserve to have your work seen and bought."

Since whatever question he'd had didn't seem important, I ignored the look and basked in how his kind words sent a warm flush flowing through me. Once more, I wanted to tell him I was falling for him, but I bit back the phrase and replied, "Thanks. I appreciate you saying that."

"No problem. It's true." He put down the painting. "Listen, I've been thinking. I want you to move up to the ranch. I'll rent a cabin for you. Stay there, with me, for a while. At least until the restraining order is in place, and we know it's been served to Chad. I'd feel better knowing the law is on your side before you're alone here again."

"That'd be some commute for me."

"True, but you don't have class every day, right? And I'd be going with you at least once a week."

"No, I don't have a full load." I thought about his request for a moment. Chad had been particularly persistent lately, and after the time Gavin and I just spent together, I wanted more. It didn't take me long to come up with an answer for him. "Sure. I'll stay on the ranch for a while. It'll give us a chance to be near each other. Plus, I really don't want to find out what Chad would do to me without you around."

CHAPTER SIX

Two weeks passed by in blissful contentment. For the most part, I'd moved in with Gavin into the rental cabin. On the days I had class, I'd return to my house to grab my mail, switch out clothes, and exchange art supplies or drop off new pieces I'd created. When Gavin had to model, he was kind enough to drive, which kept some of the mileage off my old car.

Thankfully, the people running the ranch didn't mind my continued presence there. They seemed happy with me volunteering to help where needed when I could. The horses had grown accustomed to me, and now seemed pleased when I entered the stables. Probably because I brought treats with me.

On my days away from the university, when I wasn't busy with administrative work or grading and such, I assisted Gavin with the horses' training in the rings, feeding them, and even helped with the stalls' maintenance and going out on tours. Every time I went riding, I was amazed at the beauty of the area and how it differed from the glitz and glam of the city.

Gavin had kept at me about the restraining order. I'd kept telling him I would get around to going downtown to file for it. Thing was, I hadn't seen Chad since the day he showed up on my doorstep, and Gavin had told him to get lost. Chad had sent several texts and left a few voicemails, but they'd read and sounded like the ravings of a drunk lunatic, whining about lost love and wanting to reconnect. He lamented, too, on how we didn't manage to keep our date. I was just happy he'd finally seemed to get the message that we were no longer an item.

I felt safe up on the ranch with Gavin protecting me. At the school, I'd seen Gavin's friend, Zach, hanging around. Both of us pretended not to notice the other. I figured if Gavin called in a favor to help keep an eye on me and make sure Chad didn't try anything, I wouldn't make a big deal about Zach *stalking* me. I was also sure Zach knew all about Chad and his latest communications, because I'd told Gavin about all of them.

But, today, after work and before I returned to the ranch, I filed the paperwork against Chad.

For the first time in months, I'd felt like nothing bad was waiting around the corner, that Chad had finally become the distant person and memory I'd wanted him to be. And every look and touch Gavin and I shared, and every night we spent together, I fell harder and harder for the cowboy. It was as if I'd found my best friend, my lover...my other half, and I was truly living for the first time in my life.

Wanting to see my man, I hurried back to the ranch after my morning class and trip downtown and found him shirtless and dusty, putting a colt through its paces in one of the rings, getting it to tolerate a harness and learn basic commands. The sun beat down on Gavin, making beads of sweat on his tan skin glisten in the golden light.

I loved watching him work and pulled out my phone to snap some pictures. The moment I got him into frame, he'd halted the young horse, and looked out at some distant point. A classic pose, reminding me of the cowboys of old when the west was still rugged and untamed. I thumbed the white circle, the phone clicked, then I opened the photo.

God had been generous when he'd doled out positive attributes to him. Not only was he handsome, charming, and kind to animals, he was kind to people as well. He hadn't been lying when he'd said he loved to help others. After dealing with Chad's narcissism, Gavin's generosity and caring was a pleasant change. Gavin also had an intelligence and wit about him that I enjoyed. It made our conversations and debates lively.

That wasn't to say he didn't have any negative qualities. The man could be stubborn. He left dirty socks in small piles in the bedroom and bathroom, and after being on his feet and in boots all day, they could get really rank. But those were minor details compared to what I used to have to deal with.

The fact that I felt happy and secure allowed me to release my creativity, too. Art projects poured out of me in my spare time. A few paintings I'd done of the ranch and surrounding area, I'd donated to the owners. All the rest, I'd taken back home to store in hopes that someday they'd be gracing the walls of a gallery.

In the meantime, I was enjoying my days and nights on the ranch.

Especially the nights.

Heat bloomed in my cheeks.

"That's a lovely shade of pink."

Startled, I jerked and shoved my phone in my pocket. I glanced at Gavin. "Pardon?"

"Your cheeks. They're pink. I usually only see you blush like that when we're talking about certain sexy things." He tipped back his hat and lifted an eyebrow. "Your phone. You took a picture of me again, didn't you, and were staring at it?" He stepped forward.

"I… Uh…"

He drew even closer.

Breathing deep, I took in his scent. Sun. Man. Leather. Earthy. Every feminine nerve and hormone within me went bonkers. I fought the urge to scream, "Take me! Here! Now!"

Gavin cupped my cheek. Our gazes clashed. Hot passion swelled within his. "Having some naughty thoughts again, are you, Arianna?" The corner of Gavin's mouth turned up.

Why does my name have to roll off his lips like that? All warm honey and sinfully rich fudge-like? My mouth went dry. I could only nod.

"So, it's true." He moved in and placed his mouth near my ear. "If you keep looking at me like a piece of steak you want to sink your teeth into, I won't be able to keep my hands off you."

"Then don't try," I choked out.

"Okay." He glanced at the lead in his hand, then his sexy mouth curved into a devastating smile. "Come with me while I put Little Guy away."

I followed Gavin to the stables, wondering what he had in mind. Maybe a replay of what we'd started in the barn a couple of weeks ago?

He secured Little Guy in a stall, turned, and set his sights on me. Before I could ask anything, he took off his hat and tossed it to the pile. Then he slipped his hand around the back of my head and yanked me to him, planting his mouth upon mine.

It was another world-stopping kiss in a long list of many we'd shared. I sank into him, feeling the heat of the day radiating off his body, and smoothing my hands across his slick muscles. Without breaking the kiss, he directed me into one of the clean stalls and backed me up against the wall. After a minute of making out, he pulled away, tugged at my shirt, and had it off me in a second.

Gavin feathered his lips across the tops of my breasts. "I missed you this morning. I'm sorry I've had to go out in the wee hours so many times this week."

"I get it. You take your volunteer work very seriously. I find it commendable."

"Yeah, but when I'm aching for you, it sucks." He placed his hand across my bra and cradled a mound.

"Well, we're together now," I said on a shaky breath, wishing I could feel his palm on my breast instead of through my clothing.

"That we are." In a quick move, he reached behind me, unsnapped the hooks, relieved me of my undergarment, and began to suckle on a nipple.

Loving how he knew what I was thinking, all other thoughts fled my mind, and any that did try to return only concerned him and the lusty feelings he elicited within me.

As he kept his mouth latched onto a breast, he unfastened my jeans and started to tug them down along with my panties underneath. When he couldn't reach any farther, he stopped sucking. "I want to taste you, Ari. Feel you come against my tongue. Hear you moan my name." With those words, he pushed my clothes down, brought one of my legs out of them, then draped the extremity over his shoulder.

Gavin nestled his head between my legs and placed a feather-light kiss on the top of my pussy. My nerves trilled with elation as he opened me with his fingers, flicked my clit with his tongue, and then dipped it over and between my folds. The scrape of his stubble against my sensitive skin aroused me to greater heights.

"God, you're wet for me and taste so sweet."

The hot breath fanning against me made me moan. Once again, he nipped at my sensitive nub and lapped my slit. I writhed against the wall. The rough wood scratched my back, but that bit of discomfort only added to the thrill of what we were doing. I pushed against him, encouraging him to go deeper.

Picking up on my desire, Gavin slid a couple of fingers into me. In and out they moved as he alternated between using them and his tongue. My pussy milked him as small spasms ran through me. Squirming from his arousing attention, I threaded my fingers into his hair and clenched the locks.

"I want you inside of me, Gavin."

He moved from between my legs, and with a grin, slinked up my body. "Sure thing, darlin'." As he began to unfasten his jeans, voices sounded outside the barn. "Shit. Really? Thought we'd have more time. Hurry. Get your clothes back on. I'll head out and make sure they don't come in. The door to the left of the tack tables leads to a room with an exit. Slip out that way and go to the cabin. I'll get there when I can." He rushed out of the building.

I don't think I'd ever dressed and ran out of a place so fast in my life.

Disappointment warred with excitement in me. It would have been my first time getting it on in a semi-public place, along with on the hay. The thought of getting caught was thrilling, but what if it were Kent out there, and he'd walked in on us again? Or the manager on duty, Dakota, and his friend whom I'd waved at. Gavin could have lost his job. That wouldn't have been good.

After I entered the cabin, I ran a brush through my hair, checked my clothes for dirt, and grabbed a bottled water out of the small refrigerator near the bathroom. The arousal I'd been feeling cooled with each passing minute Gavin didn't return. I sat at the small table and waited.

About half an hour later, Gavin finally strolled in. "Sorry it took me so long to get back. Kent brought a rider in off the trail. Seems she got spooked with the height of the horse and narrow paths. Then my phone blew up."

"What's going on? I was afraid we might have been seen, and you were getting your ass chewed out or fired."

"Nope. No one saw us as far as I know. But before I tell you my news, I have to ask—"

"Did I get the restraining order?" I interjected since this was how our conversations had started most days when I got back to the ranch. "I'm pleased to tell you, yes, I have."

His gaze narrowed whether in irritation that I interrupted or that it'd taken me so long to get the order, I couldn't guess.

"Good," he stated. "I've been worried that Chad might be planning something, or that he may have learned where you've been and would confront you here. And if you hadn't gone, I would have finally dragged you to the station myself to make sure you got it done."

"Sure you would've." I snorted. "Kind of like having Zachary follow me around campus?"

"That's for your own safety." Gavin all but growled.

I sighed, hating that we were barking at each other when we'd been so loving just a little while ago. "I understand that. Which is why I haven't said anything. And, I appreciate you having your friend help, especially since he should be on vacation. But I know Chad. If he hasn't done anything by now and hasn't been around, I believe he's finally done with me." I stood, reached out, and smoothed a finger over Gavin's forehead.

Gavin appeared to relax, and the horizontal lines over his eyes disappeared. "I hope to God you're right." He gave me a quick hug. "Enough of Chad for now. I have some good news for you."

"What is it?"

"I've touched base with a friend who owed me a favor. They were able to call in a couple of their own favors. How does a show sponsored by Luc and Neil Art Emporium sound?"

"Seriously?" I wanted to pinch myself to make sure I was awake. "You've secured gallery space for me there?"

"Not exactly. They're going to co-sponsor something here. An impromptu show in the tower."

"Oh."

"I'd thought you'd be more excited. You have all the ranch and tower guests who'll come. People who normally wouldn't travel all the way into San Antonio will come from nearby ranches and towns. It's a start. Isn't it?"

Gavin was right. It was a start. I'd have eyes on my work. People would learn my name. Exposure was the name of the game. I hugged him. "I'm sorry. This *is* wonderful. Thank you." I leaned back and gazed into his gorgeous eyes. "Did they say when?"

"Um…" His gaze darted away from mine.

"Um, what?" Stomach dropping and clenching, I released him and stepped back. "Please tell me it's not like a year or more from now."

"No. Nothing like that. It's in three nights."

"Three nights? As in *three* three?" My heart dropped to join my stomach. That was too soon. As much as I appreciated the gesture, the stress of getting everything done would kill me.

He nodded again.

"Damn. It doesn't leave me much time to choose my pieces, secure catering, do invites and spread the word. Hopefully the short notice doesn't keep my friends and family from being able to come out." I mentally shook my head, stopping any anxiety from taking over. I couldn't let the drawbacks stop me from seizing the chance to let clientele see my art. I'd make do like I always did and make it all work.

"Don't worry about all that. The art people and hotel staff said they'll take care of everything. All you need to do is show up with your pieces, be there to talk about your process, and answer any questions the patrons might have." He pulled his phone out of his jeans. "I'm going to text you the details I have. The contact there has your number. She'll be calling to go over things with you." His thumbs brushed over the bottom of the screen.

My phone chimed. The text appeared. "Thank you for all this." I hugged him again and snuggled into his embrace. "God, I love you." The quiet words slipped out of my mouth before I could stop them. Not that I didn't mean them. I did. I wondered if he'd heard me since I'd said them into his chest. Whether he had or not, when he didn't say anything in return, it got me thinking. Had I spoken too soon? Had his *growing love* for me been a bunch of bull? Was what was developing between us only in *my* mind?

Gavin kissed the top of my head then backed away. "I'd love to spend more time with you, but I have to get back to work." He seemed as skittish as Little Guy being harnessed and led around the ring.

I couldn't help but feel a little disappointed. When we first met and started dating, Gavin had seemed more than excited to see me and hook up with me. But now? I felt like he couldn't get away from me fast enough.

But all that was silly, right? We'd had sex almost every day. He'd gotten me set up with one of my dream galleries. If he didn't want to be with me, would he have done all that?

Damn Chad for making me paranoid when it comes to relationships.

"All right," I said, shoving my worries down. "Since I'm on a time crunch, I need to get home, decide the theme of my show, and start bringing my pieces up here. I'll talk to you later?"

"Yeah. Later." He kissed my cheek and then left the cabin.

Puzzled, I stared at the door. I'd mentioned going back to my house, and he had no comment about it? Like getting the order automatically made me bulletproof or something?

Shaking my head, I pushed all my thoughts aside and went into the bedroom. For now, I wanted to concentrate on the fact that I had a show. I packed up my dirty clothes. I'd go home, come up with a concept out of the art pieces I already had completed, do laundry, and try not to obsess about those three little words I'd said.

CHAPTER SEVEN

The afternoon of the show came upon me with a vengeance. I was so busy, I barely had time to think about eating, let alone the fact that I hadn't seen or spoken to Gavin since I'd blurted out loving him, and he left the cabin.

Three. Little. Words.

Yet they had so much power, they could change lives.

My internal chatter had me believing he'd heard me after all. Had my telling him I loved him changed everything? Part of me felt as if my world had tipped on its axis. After having hung out with Gavin so much, it felt odd not talking to or seeing him. Texting didn't seem to be a satisfactory way to communicate for me, and somehow, I kept missing him around the ranch. He wasn't coming back to the cabin in the evenings either. The other part of me was screaming that I had to focus on myself. I needed to prepare for the evening and get everything up to the banquet room in the tower.

The contact from Luc's had everything under control. So much so, I hadn't had to do much. I brought my pieces to the building, and she said the worker bees would set them all up. I asked if I needed to follow up with the restaurant downstairs since they were catering the event. She said they already had. When it came to the marketing and invites, the worker bees had handled all that as well. I'd only had to give them a list of people I knew, and they added them to their master contact list.

It was all very efficient. I almost felt left out of my own gig.

I also didn't like feeling that my show might be "less than" if Gavin didn't attend. During a text conversation, he hadn't said he wasn't coming. But then, he hadn't confirmed he was.

Once more, I tried to call him. It went straight to voicemail.

Somehow, I had to find the courage to ask if he'd heard what I'd said the other day and see if he was ignoring me or something.

My stomach tied into a knot. I grabbed a can of ginger ale out of the fridge. I didn't have time for nerves or queasiness. I needed to get to the salon in the tower to get my hair, make-up, and nails done, then come back, get into my dress, and get to the show.

* * * *

A few hours later, I was all dolled up. I'd missed Gavin's call while getting my hair done, but he assured me he'd be at the show and apologized profusely that he hadn't been around more to support me and help me get ready for my event. I was just happy I'd heard from him, and he wasn't lying in a ditch somewhere. His call also helped to silence my inner voice and doubts about him.

After one last check in the mirror to make sure I was ready, I took a deep breath and left the cabin. At the tower, I went in through the administration doors as I'd been instructed to do and up the employee elevator to the floor where the multi-use rooms were. To avoid seeing people waiting to get into the show so the numbers, or lack thereof, wouldn't make me nervous, I walked through a back of the house hallway and into the venue through an employee only door.

A large conference room had been set up with white drapery hiding the walls. The satiny sheets also curved down from the ceiling in graceful arcs with twinkle lights spread out beneath them, sparkling like stars from above. Large wood boards painted white were set up like temporary walls, creating a maze in the room and displaying my works of art.

The sign near the main doors read *Luc and Neil Art Emporium presents Arianna Perez*, and the pamphlets of info on a table at the front highlighted pictures of the gallery, information on the gallery staff and on me, and the gallery's San Antonio location. I grabbed a couple of the printouts so I could send them to my parents and *abuela* since they couldn't make it.

Taking some time before the event opened to the public, I strolled through the maze. On the walls, my artwork looked more elegant than I ever imagined it could with the appropriate arrangements and lighting. The theme of the evening was *The Journey*, what one could see and who they could meet during travels and in dreams. Most of the pieces were in the style of abstract impressionism—landscapes, seascapes, animals, still lifes. Some others had a more realism aspect about them while others went to total abstraction. There was even a large portrait of Gavin I'd done.

As I took a moment to breathe, to silently express my gratitude for the opportunity, and to snap some photos for my parents, Tyler strolled up to me.

"Professor Perez? Are you ready?" he asked, indicating the hotel staff member standing at the doors about to let the people in.

"Yes. As ready as I'll ever be." I moved to a spot between the food and DJ. This way the clients could meander through the show and assess the art without my intrusion. Should they wish an audience with the artist—this time me—then a staff member or Tyler would make the introductions.

To my delight, people seemed to keep filing into the space. I recognized a few—the ones from my list—and Gavin's buddy, Zachary. He joined a small group. Probably more of Gavin's friends Zach had been introduced to during his visit. But no sight of Gavin.

I grabbed a flute of champagne off the tray of a passing waiter and sipped on the bubbly liquid, taking in the sights and sounds around me. Tyler waved me over to a couple who were looking at my "Tide Pool" piece. After several minutes of talking to them about my process and teaching position, I was introduced to another patron and then a third, and even one of the wranglers wanted a piece for him and his girlfriend. Soon, my throat started feeling like Death Valley in the middle of July. I excused myself and went over to the food table to find some water.

"Arianna Perez. Lovely to see you."

Drawing my attention away from the appetizers, I looked toward the owner of the melodic voice. The older woman seemed familiar, but I couldn't place her. Then she smiled and laugh lines formed around her blue eyes. Gavin's mother, Rosalyn Bishop. I'd thought her to be pretty with her dark hair and porcelain skin when I was younger. Now? She was stunning and seemed to be aging very well. "Mrs. Bishop. What a surprise! Thank you so much for coming out for my show."

She gave me a slight smile. "You're welcome. Though, I'm here more for my Gavin. It's been over a year since he's been home to see us."

A year? Was that what Gavin had meant by "a while ago" when he'd mentioned how long he'd been back in Texas? But her presence would explain why I hadn't seen him in the past few days. I was about to ask if they'd been having a nice time together when she continued talking.

"He tells me the two of you are dating?" A pinched expression came to her face. "I don't think I approve. You've always been a nice person. Respectful. Intelligent. Kind. But the age difference. His father and I want grandchildren, and well, you're reaching that point where..." she glanced toward my abdomen so fast I almost missed the look, "*things*...aren't so viable anymore."

I couldn't help gasping. "I'm not that old. Just nearing thirty-four, and my *things* are just fine," I remarked, not missing her insinuation. "If Gavin and I—" I stopped talking when I realized she wasn't listening. Rosalyn focused on a point across the room. I tracked my gaze in the same direction. Gavin stood with the group of people I'd assumed were his friends.

Why hadn't he come over to say hello to me? Had Rosalyn told him her concerns between the last time I saw him and now? Maybe I'd been right to be skeptical about us getting together due to our ages, and whether a relationship was worth pursuing. What if my *things* really weren't fine? I wouldn't want to ruin his dreams and cause problems between him and his family just because I couldn't conceive.

"But then with his *career*," Rosalyn went on, "maybe having a wife and children isn't a good idea. He loves his work, but I don't see how playing around on a ranch could support a family. But then, I feel safer with him here than out on patrol and working undercover trying to make detective. I'm just glad my sweet boy hadn't become cynical and guarded like his co-workers and hadn't been harmed in the line of duty before he left." She tossed a glare my way. "It's all your fault really. He loved it when you came over and kept watch over him and Cassady. Thought it was admirable how you liked to help people. He wanted to do the same. Even after we moved, you were the most important thing to him. I can't tell you how many times his father and I tried to set him up with other women, only to see those relationships dissolve within a matter of weeks. You. It's always only been you."

Her words, coated with a criticizing tone, barely registered, except for the ones regarding work—patrol, undercover... "A cop?" My stomach felt like it was clenching around white-hot rocks. I couldn't seem to take a deep breath. "He... He works on a ranch. He's a wrangler. He's been modeling in one of my classes."

He's been asking me loads of questions about Chad and keeping tabs on me.

Am I part of an investigation?

"Oh, dear." The older woman placed her fingers in front of her mouth. Her eyes widened. "I wasn't supposed to say anything."

Trying to keep my stomach in check and not become a crazy banshee, I looked back at the group. "Would you please excuse me, Mrs. Bishop?"

"Of course."

I headed through the throng of people toward Gavin and his friends. As I neared, I slowed and then stopped to listen to their conversation. From the snippets I caught, I surmised that they'd been working to get evidence regarding a pair of brothers who partook in organized crime. One of the leaders happened to be overseeing a front in San Antonio— Luc and Neil Art Emporium. Chad was a lackey, basically doing anything they asked. They had word the brothers were on the move and heading to Texas and hoped the pair, or their workers—or all of them—would show up at the gallery and do something so the team could bust them.

Gavin looked like he kept trying to get a word in but didn't have much luck.

Not that I cared. The excitement and happiness I'd felt earlier in the evening completely disappeared, replaced with utter disappointment.

My art show had been a set-up. It was bait.

I'd been used.

Lied to.

Again.

Though I wanted to storm up to Gavin and give him a piece of my mind, I knew I needed to gather myself. There was no way I could confront him here in a rational frame of mind, and *here* was the last place I wanted to make a scene. I hurried to the administrative offices where I could sneak downstairs and out the back door for some air.

Out behind the tower and ranch lodge, I bent over, hands on my knees, and breathed. On one of our trail rides, I'd told Gavin that honesty and trust were the two biggest qualities I looked for in a relationship. He'd said he felt the same. But he'd done the exact opposite. He hadn't trusted me to tell me what was going on. He'd lied to me by omission. What should have been one of the happiest nights of my life was turning into an absolute nightmare.

"You fucking bitch." The words were slurred, but the voice was unmistakable.

"Go away, Chad," I said without looking up from the ground, "before I call the cops and tell them you're breaking the restraining order." Maybe Gavin was right. Chad could definitely be on something.

He spat at me. The wad of spittle jiggled on the pavement near my feet.

"You and your cop friends. You ruined me. I had a great thing going. They planned to promote me in the organization. But no! That asshole you're seeing... His buddies came sniffing around. You couldn't keep your mouth shut, could you? The big boss told me I was a liability. Said I couldn't be trusted because I couldn't control my woman. Beat me for my troubles and kicked me out of the biz. But, luckily, being here tonight and giving them a quick call with some great intel might have gotten me back into their good graces."

"Keep my mouth shut? I don't know anything to tell. You know what? I'm glad they beat you. Give you a taste of your own medicine." I looked up and shot him the evilest glare I could muster.

Chad howled and came at me, fingers extended and bent like claws.

Before I could fully straighten up, he grabbed my hair and yanked, exposing the front of my body to his fist. Punch after punch pounded my stomach, my chest, my sides. I tried to turn away and lash out at Chad, as Gavin had taught me to do for this particular situation in one of our short lessons, but Chad seemed to anticipate my moves. He tightened his hold and didn't allow me to escape.

Furious and fearing for my life, I wanted to fight back, to scream and alert someone, but the air had left my lungs. Without oxygen, I was immobile. His fist connected to my face. Bones crackled. Searing hot pain lanced through my head. He shoved me to the ground and started to kick me. Through an agonizing, knife-like, stabbing fog, I had enough wherewithal of thought to curl into a ball.

As he whacked me, I caught a sufficient breath to yell at him to stop. He laughed and spouted a bunch of gibberish, but I did understand some of the insults and vile names he called me.

Here was a man who'd said he'd loved me. Now, I was going to die by his hands and feet. My vision and hearing dimmed, but I could have sworn I saw a man with a shovel take a swing at Chad's head. Someone—the man?—was telling me to get up, to run.

I couldn't go out this way, like a beaten animal in a gutter. Fighting for my life, I put my hands on the ground and tried to push myself up, but all my strength fled from my muscles. I collapsed onto the asphalt. Fluid filled my mouth, leaving behind a metallic taste. Overcome with pain and a strong desire to sleep, I closed my eyes.

From what sounded like a great distance away, Chad cackled.

Someone—the man?—apologized, saying he tried and sorry he wasn't able to help.

Then I heard the pounding of footfalls and shouts.

"Get away from her."

"Put your hands in the air."

"Arianna!"

Gavin. Gavin was here. He'd protect me, right? He'd promised he'd keep me safe.

The voices grew fainter.

"Stop!"

Chad's assault ended. His feet shuffled against the pavement near me. Again, he shouted something unintelligible.

"Drop the weapon!"

"Don't come closer, or I'll shoot her!"

My ex had a gun?

I sure as hell didn't want to find out what a bullet wound would feel like. As I took in a shuddering breath to ask for help, the last thing I remember was the powerful, echoing crack of a firearm.

CHAPTER EIGHT

Beeps. Dings. Pings. Static.

The incessant rhythmic noises stabbed my mind.

Discomfort poked at my hand and twisted around my arm.

I didn't like the irritations. I wanted to go back into the fog, into the quiet void of nothingness, where my body didn't hurt, and my mind was at rest. Soon I thankfully drifted back into the cradle of darkness.

Moments later, or so it seemed, I had vague notions of hearing people—my parents, Gavin, strangers, but I didn't know where or when. Mostly, I'd been feeling as if I'd been on a cloud just floating in the breeze. My face and head hurt again along with my throat this time. I took a breath that felt like it was full of razor blades, but soon that eased. Still, I didn't want to wake yet, regardless of what the voices on the wind were saying.

No. Not yet. Not ready to face the light.

Sometime later, a quiet pleading voice broke into my silent, dark space. I didn't want to open my eyes, yet that voice kept telling me I had to. So, I did. Slowly, I came to.

Gavin stood over me as I lay staring up at him. Worry lines creased his face. His eyes looked red. As if he'd been crying.

"Hospital?" I croaked out in a raspy whisper.

He nodded and put a cup with a straw in it near my lips. "Almost two weeks. You've been heavily sedated. Were in a medically induced coma for a bit and intubated during it."

I took a sip of room temperature water, and was about to draw some more into my mouth, when he pulled it away from me.

"But you'll be okay in time." Gavin brought a chair closer to the side of the bed and sat. "You had us all worried there for a while. That fucking bastard sure did a number to you."

That's when the memories of the evening came back in full force. The show. Mrs. Bishop. The lies. Chad. "You..." I swallowed hard, cleared my throat. "You lied to me."

"Ari—"

"Don't Ari me."

A nurse came in and shooed him out of the room. I shifted to try to get a better position in the uncomfortable bed and winced from a sharp pain in my side. It seemed my torso was wrapped in bandages. Most likely from broken ribs. My nose throbbed, too. Probably busted.

"Relax, Miss Perez. You're healing well. The doctor will be in to see you soon."

A couple hours later the doctor arrived, informed me of my fractures, cuts, bruises, and that they'd sedated me to help keep me calm and motionless so I could start the healing process. We determined that to continue keeping me calm, I shouldn't have visitors for a bit. I really wanted to talk to Gavin but knew it'd be for the best if I was alone to rest.

A few days later, he was the first person back to see me.

"I can't believe they wouldn't let me in here. I'm sorry. I tried to see you, but—"

Holding up my hand, I made him stop talking. "I know. The doctor and I thought it best I have no visitors. I didn't need the stress. But now that I'm doing somewhat better..." I looked at the chair and tipped my chin toward it, indicating he should sit. "I still have something to say."

"Is this about you thinking I lied? But I never lied to you."

"You lied by omission. You didn't tell me you were using me to help your friends get at

Chadwick. That your *buddies* were with law enforcement. That y'all were working on bringing down an organized crime family. Was that all I was to you? Some kind of pawn so you and your friends could get a job done? Has everything we shared been lies?"

Gavin shook his head. "No. God no. You're not a pawn. You weren't bait." He gently picked up my hand and gave it a light squeeze. "You're my love, my everything. I've meant every word I've ever said. I've cherished every second we've spent together. I wanted to tell you I love you after you said it, but then I started to worry. How would you react when you learned about my past job and what my friends requested of me? When they learned I knew you, they thought it'd be an easy way to get some inside information. But what if you or I got hurt during all this? Then my mom showed up. Those days when I couldn't get away from her and see you or talk to you on the phone? They were difficult. I realized I hated being apart from you. I love you. I can't live without you."

Could I believe him? After everything that'd happened, could I believe anyone ever again? I'd come close to dying. If Gavin had trusted me, been up front with me, I could have protected myself by going to visit my parents or taken a "vacation" like the other professor.

"You were making my decisions for me. You should have been upfront and let me decide all that for myself." I breathed as deep as the cloth constraints allowed and let the breath out in a sigh. "The day we created the painting together... It didn't even click when you mentioned the humanities courses. Your taking a few classes here and there was something more. You've been to college. You have a degree, don't you, Gavin?"

"Yes." He bowed his head. "I have a master's in criminal justice with a background in psychology and political science."

"Great." I shifted in the bed. Now that I was fully awake and getting more restless with each day, I found the thin mattress to be uncomfortable. "What else is there that you haven't told me?"

"Well—"

"*Dios mío.*" I snatched my hand out of his. "There is more? Please don't tell me your mom lied to me, too, and you're married."

"I'm not. I wouldn't have let our relationship develop that far if I had been. I'm not a cheater."

I shot him a glare. "What relationship between us? Everything you've told me has been a lie."

"Again, Arianna, that's not true. My feelings and thoughts about you have all been real. Just kept some of my background and how long I've been back in Texas from you. I did work on ranches and on rescue crews out in CA, but I moved to Las Vegas about three years ago and joined the force there. I realized being a cop wasn't my true passion. I do live at Gateway. My cousin and his wife did leave and that's how I got the gig. I like working on the ranch because I enjoy being outside and working with the animals, plus it gives me a place to stay. I still do rescue work. Yes, I went to college and grad school. And, the professor you replaced? He'd been sent on an indefinite, paid vacation by my friends. This way you could be put in place, and they could arrange my meeting you. Nothing's happened to him. He's probably enjoying Mai Tais on a tropical isle somewhere."

I huffed and turned my head away. Words. Just lots of words.

Gavin fingered my chin and made me look at him again. His steady gaze drilled into mine. "Everything I've felt about you, said about you, and to you on a personal level, all that's been true. When the team arranged for the other professor to take a vacation and have you take over the class, they'd planned to put another man into the modeling position—"

"Let me guess. Russo?" Zach looked like he could have modeled for a big agency.

"Yeah, and he hated the idea. When I'd learned it was you who was mixed up with Chad, I knew I had to make sure you'd be all right. They didn't want me to do it, but I'd convinced them I'd be perfect for the job. Told them that because we once knew each other, it'd be easy for me to enter your world, gain your trust, and keep an eye on you, and thus Chad indirectly. They didn't know about my feelings for you at first, or else they definitely wouldn't have let me try. But, they gave me the chance. Told me to keep an eye on you and gather any bit of intel I could on Chadwick Hayes that would help lead us to the organization's kingpins."

"That explains all the questions and your theories."

Gavin shrugged. "It was tough trying to be discreet yet hunt for information. Even harder when my love for you kept growing. When I'd learned you were still in San Antonio… God, I was so happy. Never had the others or I thought Chadwick was causing you harm. After the incident in the hall, we'd tried to keep an eye on you the best we could."

"Right. Zachary. But you'd said you couldn't track me down. You were on the force. You had sources that can be used to find people. If you've thought of me over the years as you said you had, you could have used the means to find me ages ago." If he had, I might have avoided years of agony with Chad. I wouldn't have ended up in this bed, beat to hell. "Why didn't you?"

"My mother. She knew how hung up on you I'd been and still was, and she'd told me you'd moved with your parents toward the gulf. Why would I doubt her? So, I didn't abuse my powers to search the venues at my disposal to locate you. I'm kicking myself for not even trying. I could have saved you a world of hurt. I could have kept you safe. I—"

"Stop, Gavin." I studied his face. He seemed contrite and remorseful. I couldn't bring myself to make him feel worse by continuing to accuse him of lying. Plus, I realized he had tried, in his own way, to keep me safe and had been transparent with me as much as he could. "There's no saying I would have broken up with Chad back then to be with you. The timing *for us* would have been wrong then."

"If only you'd introduced him to Chavela."

I chuckled then grimaced at the pain in my abdomen the action caused. "True. She would have had a field day reading him and warned me off of him from the start." Not looking forward to the time when I'd have to spook Gavin and let him know that Chavela's *skills* had been passed down, I tried to stretch my torso but didn't have much movement. Somehow, I'd have to find a way to tell him about the gardener trying to rescue me, and that his grandfather was wanting to talk. Since I had other stuff to deal with, I told his relative he'd have to wait. Too bad the spirits couldn't have warned me about my own life. Soon though, I'd have to face the hard fact that for some reason I'd been totally blind and deaf in all aspects—instinctually, literally, psychically—when it'd come to Chad, which only added to my shame for not being and feeling smarter in that man's regard. But as *Abuela* would say, *Nothing happens without reason.* "As much as I hate being in this hospital bed, everything most likely happened as it should have."

"But still. You shouldn't be here." He waved a hand at the bed. "Believe me, many times I'd wanted to tell you what was going on, but I couldn't jeopardize the operation and all the months of work the detectives had done. But if I could do it over again…" He paused, bowed his head, and took a shaky breath. "They had to try to get evidence fast… Then they'd lost track of Chad. When I'd heard he showed up at the hotel, and then my mother ran up to me, saying you'd gone outside because she'd slipped and told you my background… And then seeing you and him out back… I…" He choked back a breath. "I nearly lost my mind." He squeezed his eyes shut and clenched his hands.

"A gun. I remember one being fired. Obviously, it wasn't at me. What happened?"

Gavin opened his eyes and looked at me, but he didn't seem to see me. "Chad was shot. The officers were carrying. They believed he would have killed you. The officer who fired aimed for center of mass, but Chad had moved, and the bullet only winged him. I had to be restrained from attacking him and giving him a beating like he'd dealt you...or worse even. God, I was fit to be tied. Russo reminded me the last thing you'd need is Chad getting off due to assault. He's in police custody now and won't be getting out any time soon. There were enough witnesses that he can't charm his way out of all the charges."

Gavin's breath grew shaky. He took my hand again, leaned forward, resting his elbows on the edge of the bed, and held the backs of my fingers to his forehead. "I feel like I broke my promise to you to keep you safe. If you had died..." After a long, faltering breath, he sniffled. "It... It would have killed me."

Any lingering anger I held slipped away. The only feeling remaining was the love that I had for him. I turned my fingers and gripped his hand as tight as I could. "It's all right. I see your side. You did the best you could under odd circumstances. Now at least Chad's somewhere where he can't hurt me. Or come after you, which was probably going through his mind at some point as something to do."

Gavin offered a small smile, rose from the chair, leaned over and kissed my forehead. "I am so grateful you're okay, and that you're in my life. I have something for you." He reached behind him and pulled out an envelope from his pocket. "Here."

"What's this?" The upper left corner had the name and address of the gallery on it.

"Open it." Gavin sat. "Almost all your pieces sold. That's the payment from the gallery. Fortunately, it was one of the legitimate businesses, so the check is good and not part of the frozen assets. My mom also wants to apologize for what she'd said. She'd filled me in on your conversation. She's just trying to protect me and make sure I'm not making mistakes. I told her my profession and loving you aren't mistakes. She claims she's happy for me. For us. When you're up for more visitors, she'll be here in person to tell you all this."

"That'll be nice." I wasn't sure I wanted to see her, but I'd at least listen to what she had to say. I slid the check from the envelope. "Oh my God. This is mine?"

"Yep. All yours. I gather it's good?"

Dumfounded, I stared at the numbers on the blue-and-white paper. *Nine grand.* A nice chunk of change for a relative nobody in the art world. "Yes. Yes, it's fabulous. Thank you so much for helping me get the show."

"You're welcome. From what I understand, there should be a letter in there, too."

I looked back in the envelope and pulled out the folded paper I'd thought was just an invoice. I had to read it twice before the information sunk in. Tears welled in my eyes.

"Ari? What? What's wrong?"

"Nothing's wrong. Everything's fine. Great actually. The hotel wants a series of commissioned pieces. Large ones. Like the ones in my show. Those, along with this check, will help me pay off my student loans." I clutched all the items in my hands to my chest. "Oh, Gavin, thank you. You don't know how much all this means to me. I wish I could get out of bed and show you how much."

He chuckled and gave the charming smile that'd always made me weak in the knees. "There'll be time for all that after you're healed. In fact, I hope we'll have the rest of our lives to show each other how much."

I raised a brow. "Are you saying, or rather asking, what I think you are?"

"Perhaps." He winked. "For now, I want you to get some rest. This way we can spring you from this place as soon as possible. Then we can revisit this conversation."

"You're not leaving right now, are you?"

"No. I'll stay until you fall asleep. I love you, Arianna. I'll always be here to keep you safe."

Warmth filled my soul upon hearing his admission. I smiled as best I could. "I like the sound of that." Since I was no longer angry, an overwhelming tiredness swept over me. The discussion had drained me of energy. Content that all was finally right with the world—Gavin loved me and I him—I closed my eyes and drifted off into slumber.

EPILOGUE

It'd been three months since the incident at the hotel, and I was literally and figuratively back in the saddle. Gavin and I were dividing our time between living at my house in the city and our jobs there—he'd decided to continue being a model—with being up at the ranch to help with the animals and tours. I liked calling him my wrangler. Though, having him wear his skivvies during class wasn't all that bad either.

The discussion about my *skills* activating had gone better than planned. Being older and more knowledgeable about the world around him, Gavin didn't seem too fazed. In fact, he quite enjoyed the few minutes of "conversation" with his grandfather. It also helped that Dakota's girlfriend, Kat, had some of her own abilities, so the men were able to commiserate with each other while I had someone to help me learn how to ground myself and establish boundaries.

We directed our mounts up the trail to Sunset Hill where we liked to picnic. In one direction it gave a great view of the area. In the other, we enjoyed watching the brilliant sunsets when we made it in time to watch them. Today we were up there for a private lunch.

Chadwick was still in custody. Eventually, he'd have to go to trial, and I'd have to testify. Gavin informed me Chad had squealed on the brothers to make a deal for less time in jail. His information helped to add up more charges against the pair, especially considering the one brother had made an attempt to kidnap Kat. But I didn't want to think of Chad or any of that. I just wanted to focus on the man on the horse in front of me.

"Here good?" He shifted in the saddle and looked back at me.

"Perfect."

We dismounted. While I spread out a blanket on the ground and pulled the food out of the basket, he secured the horses' reins to a post that he'd put up weeks ago. As the animals grazed nearby on the sparse tufts of grass, we munched on sandwiches, and I told him about the latest commission I'd been hired to do.

"I hope you don't mind taking on another venture," Gavin said, putting down his plate and reaching into a pocket.

Between all our different projects, I hoped whatever he was thinking wouldn't take up too much of our time. "What do you have in mind? We're so busy as it is already."

"Oh, not much." He pulled out a box and flipped it open. In it sat a platinum ring with three princess cut diamonds, the middle one larger than the other two. "Just being mine forever, is all." He grinned at my squeal of delight. "Arianna Nicole Soto Perez, will you do me the honor of becoming my wife and letting me be your husband for now and always?"

My heart swelled with love for my wrangler-model. I nodded enthusiastically. "Yes. Of course, yes!"

I threw my arms around him and planted my mouth on his. As other times, it was a kiss that made my toes curl, and I looked forward to sharing many more of the same in the future.

Dear Reader ~

I'd like to talk about a couple of things.

If you're a fan and a good portion of this story seemed familiar, it's because it's been previously published. Since getting rights back, I updated and edited it. I feel that the story is new and improved due to the added scenes and re-editing. I hope you do, too. If this is the first time you're reading this version or any of my work, thank you so much for your purchase and your readership! Whether a returning fan or newbie, remember to help show your support of authors by leaving reviews. This includes leaving a review of this book, please and thank you!

Now, on a more serious note, if you or a loved one is suffering from abuse, whether it be emotional, physical, or verbal, stemming from a family member, friend, boss/colleague, please seek help. As it states here https://www.thehotline.org/, "...highly-trained advocates are available 24/7/365 to talk confidentially with anyone experiencing domestic violence, seeking resources or information, or questioning unhealthy aspects of their relationship." Taking that first step toward safety and peace of mind may be hard, but your life, or the life of the person you know, is worth it.

A word about the author...

An eccentric and eclectic writer, C.R. Moss pens stories for the mainstream and erotic romance markets, giving readers a choice of sweet, savory or spicy reads, usually within a sub-genre or two — paranormal, sci-fi/fantasy, time travel, or western flare. She also has a passion for penning dark fiction. Writing as Casey Moss, she delves into the darker aspects of life in her work, sometimes basing the stories on reality, sometimes on myth. No matter the path, her stories will take you on a journey from the lighthearted paranormal to dark things unspeakable. What waits around the corner? Come explore…

www.caseymscorner.com

᚛᚛᚛᚛

Thank you for purchasing this publication.
If you enjoyed the story, we would appreciate your letting others know by leaving a review.
For other wonderful stories, please visit:
https://threeflamespublishing.com/

᚛᚛᚛᚛